BARE

Flash Ficti

BARE BOOKS
Volume I

Compiled by Daizi Rae

Contributing authors in order of appearance:
Carolyn Ward-Daniels
Gerry O'Keeffe
Daizi Rae
April Berry
Elaine Morris
TJ Spencer
Dean Wrigley
Jayne Love

Thank you for being part of our journey,
and for helping our charity of choice
Book Trust UK [Getting children reading]
to do even more good work

INTRODUCTION

Fifty-six different flash fiction stories means fifty-six different bite sized treats. All brand new original chunks of creativity from eight different independent authors, any of which could become your new favourite.

Based on sixteen different writing prompts, you could be amazed, amused, inspired, or afraid at the turn of a page. Flash Fiction is ideal for the waning attention span that still insists on the full story, 'less is more,' as they say. The shortest story could reveal the largest truth or the biggest emotion.

This anthology is a passion project, a natural progression from the Bare Books podcast. Dedicated to giving independent authors a free platform to talk about, and share, their writing, and raise their profile for readers old and new. The obvious next step was to take the wonderful stories we read to our listeners on the podcast, plus a sprinkling of extra stories you will not have heard, and publish them in this anthology. We will donate all profits from sales of this book to charity. Our charity of choice is the **Book Trust UK** [Getting children reading]. So, if you have bought this book, thank you.

Daizi Rae

CONTENTS

JANUARY SALES

By Carolyn Ward-Daniels

For the first time in months, Jan was cooking a proper meal. Her first Christmas day as a singleton. Her brother Brian had bullied her into hosting Christmas dinner. He'd be turning up with his wife Kate and dad. It was a first for him as well. Jan welled up thinking of her mum dying at the same time her husband walked out.

The house had the aroma of roasting turkey and her cooking skills were on trial, as she had dwindled to beans on toast to sandwiches as she couldn't be arsed to cook for just herself and she resented being forced into it now. Well, she didn't want her dad to be on his own, but why couldn't Brian invite everyone to theirs? Not that she would have gone.

Earlier, she had reluctantly fetched the tree and decorations down from the attic and trimmed up. She wouldn't have bothered if they hadn't been coming. She had to go out and do a load of shopping instead of curling up on the sofa with the quilt. Jan felt drained before they arrived but got changed into a skirt and blouse, both a bit creased but she couldn't be arsed to iron.

The knock on the door made her grimace, and she hoped they wouldn't stay all day. Her dad walked in with a smile and a bag of presents. They hugged, and he loaded Kate with home baked mince pies and a Christmas cake. Brian handed her presents, and she immediately hoped they hadn't spent a lot, as she had just bought them aftershave and perfume. Jan hadn't the heart for shopping. She didn't have any Christmas spirit in her at all.

Jan had bought her dad a cardigan, and she noticed he had filled out a bit whereas she had dropped a stone she didn't need to. The house was quiet, so Jan put the TV on and switched the fairy lights on to cheer the place up. Everyone seemed happy with their gifts, the gift of oil paints, brushes and canvass board took her by surprise, from her dad. 'You were always good at art Jan,' he said. 'It's about time you took it up again.'

Dinner was a success even though Jan was miserable inside as she busied herself fussing over the food, not eating much herself. She was pleased when they all retired to the lounge and refused any help in the kitchen, and she was relieved when they left. Closing the door behind them, then resting her back on it to shut out the world. Then she slid down to the floor and cried in silence.

The days to New Year's Eve had been blank and Jan spent a lot of time staring at nothing, thinking nothing and weeping. It was the end of a shit year, and she didn't want to start another. She zombie shuffled into the lounge, took down the cards, unplugged the tree, and carried it to the back door. She was going to dump the whole thing in the bin. The key wasn't in the door and she couldn't be arsed to search for it, so she robotically took it back to the attic. It was freezing up there, and she dumped the tree, still fully decorated, in the corner. The room had the borrowed light from a street lamp and she moved to the dormer window. There was a superb view over the Christmas lit town. It was ten o'clock, taxis were dashing around, and a gritter-lorry was coating the icy roads. Any trees with foliage were fighting a ferocious wind, and the cold made her stiffen. Then she thought that if she opened the window and sat on the ledge, she would freeze to death and slide down the roof and out of the future. The window was locked, no key in sight. 'What is it with bloody keys now!' she spat. She saw the huge banner on the department store in the square. Big white letters on a red background 'JANUARY SALE' It was tied to the guttering, and the wind made it flap violently, then the right side broke free and it flipped up and across the roof, white side up. Jan watched as it did a frantic flip, landed letter side up, and folded. It read 'JAN SALE.' It was her name, and it held her attention. It then whipped again and landed all concertina. The only clear letter was 'U' before it performed again a caterpillar arrangement spelling 'ARSE,' before somersaulting away to the floor. Jan gripped the cold windowsill. She knew she had been sent a message. 'JAN U ARSE.' She put her coat on and headed for the store. The banner hung like a bandage. In the window, there was a shabby chic painted wall panel. On it were the words 'HAPPINESS IS A JOURNEY NOT A DESTINATION,' Jan's mobile rang. It was her dad.

'I'm just ringing to wish you a Happy New Year, darlin', and make sure you live a good one. I miss your mum every day, you know, but now I can listen to jazz music when I like and I've got my saxophone out. Your mum hated both. I also have a bacon sandwich for breakfast instead of ruddy muesli.' Just as she stared at the wall panel her dad said, 'Happiness is a journey darlin', and I am going to be happy on the rest of my journey and I want to see you do the same. Oh, and that wax coat you wear, Jan, it does nothing for you, it's the colour of soil, you look like you've just been dug up. I put you £200 in the pocket. Go get yourself a nice smart coat in the January sales.'

JANUARY SALES

By Gerry O'Keeffe

New Year's Eve 1914

Kendo was lying on his back, in the hospital tent, bombs going off around him, both in his head and in the distance. His mind was tormenting him with terrifying images of the carnage he'd witnessed on the battlefield.

The foul stench of blood, sweat and rotting corpses, mixed with alcohol and disinfectant, filled his senses. Mental images of heads being severed, body parts scattered everywhere, tormented his already shattered mind.

As a new year approached, he wondered what the future held for everyone in the tent and those out in the trenches. He looked around the tent at his comrades in arms; some with missing limbs, blinded, scarred, or maimed for life. Medics fighting tirelessly to save everyone's life, rushing around grabbing supplies, bandages, cleaning gauze, alcohol to disinfect wounds.

Kendo held onto his hip flask with his shaking hands and took a swig of his rum. It calmed him down. He looked over at his friend Kolin; he was fast asleep. Kendo smiled, then beckoned the medic over and handed her the remaining contents of his hip flask, saying, 'You need this more than me.' She took a swig of the contents gratefully, then put the hip flask in her apron pocket.

The hustle and bustle of the tent reminded Kendo of the many January sales held in his memories. Instead of trading commodities, though, this time they traded lives. Instead of being near crushed in some crazy sale, they were running for their lives, with severed limbs instead of a post-Christmas bargain. Pleading with medics to save themselves and their friends coming off the battlefield.

Amid the chaos of the tent, Kendo noticed a fellow Celtic brother from bonnie Scotland, Angus Delaney, brought in. Was it only a week ago that Angus was one of the star strikers in a football match between the warring nations? They had called a truce for the day, where all men were equal in a moment of clarity, if only for that one day. Now here he was, blinded in one eye, missing part of his arm and a foot. Kendo watched the scene in front of him, his heart filled with sorrow for his friend, and his eyes filled with tears. What future did his friend have to look forward to? He had been all set to play for Liverpool football club when the war was over, so what now, he couldn't just go to the January sales and buy himself a new limb or an eye. It hurt to watch Angus in so much pain, knowing that his friend was facing so many life struggles after the war, assuming he got out of this alive.

The medic that was treating Angus felt the hip flask in her pocket, so she handed it to him to take a drink. Maybe it would help, if only a little. Kendo smiled to see this. Angus took a swig. At first, his face filled with joy from the sweet taste of the rum, but then he grimaced as a bitterness hit him. Despite this, Kendo willed his friend to drink it all. Angus reluctantly did as his friend willed, draining every drop until he fell back, blissfully passing out from the anguish that filled his pain wracked body.

Later that night, they could hear bells ringing out from outside the tent. Shouts of 'Happy New Year' heard in the distance, coming closer and closer, followed by tired, broken voices singing out the lyrics to Auld Lang Syne, and joy filled Kendo's heart. Kendo got up out of his bed and walked over to Angus, he took out a cough medicine bottle, poured whatever golden nectar was in there, the magic of Christmas maybe, into the empty hip flask that Angus was still holding, and then raised a toast to the New Year. Angus took it, drank it back, then looked into his friends eyes with both of his own, what miracle was this! Angus sat in bed watching in awe as his arm regenerated and both his feet seemed to be exactly where they should be.

From the despair of the battlefield came the Joy of a New Year celebration. Even if more war and bloodshed were to follow. There was now, and always would be, hope. Kendo thought back to other wars he had lived through, other bodies he had regenerated, mostly his own to be fair. He smiled to himself, wished Angus farewell, walked over to kiss the sleeping Kolin on the forehead and whisper him a happy new year, and vanished quietly out of the back of the tent to find his trusty TARDIS.

ALLONS-Y!

JANUARY SALES

Daizi Rae

Norman sat on the side of Jessica's bed, gazing down at the serene, sleeping face of his daughter. He sat with an erratic, elevated heart rate, the sweat slowly drying on his brow. Who would ever have guessed that the screaming tantrums of a six-year-old little girl could shake his world and his sanity to such extremes?

Norman was a desperate man; he had to do what his daughter wanted before their world imploded. He felt he might be on the verge of a heart attack, which would leave his princess at the mercy of her unreliable bitch of a mother. That or he could pack a bag and run, run for the hills and never look back. All this drama for a doll called Tina who cried 'real' tears!

As he stared down at the sleeping tyrant with the angelic face, a glimmer of a plan started forming in his mind. He knew that 'The Forgotten Toyshop' had the one remaining doll available for sale in their town, and Norman thought he knew just how to get it.

It was New Year's Eve 2019, when high street shops were still a thing. The biggest risk to going shopping was being crushed in the crowds, frantic to grab a bargain.

Just after midnight, Norman let himself into his neighbour, Millie's house. She never locked the back door. And if he knew anything, he knew that by this time she'd be snoring in a drunken stupor on the sofa. The joys of single parent life, celebrating New Year alone at home. Norman spirited himself upstairs. Picked up Millie's son, four-year-old Fletcher and carried him, still sleeping, back to his own house. He gently carried him upstairs and tucked him into bed, then he padded back downstairs and locked the front and back doors.

He settled himself at the kitchen table where he took a certain amount of joy ripping letters carefully out of newspapers and magazines, arranging them into a ransom note, just as he'd seen on his favourite show, Murder She Wrote. The finished note read like this:

'I have your son. If you want to see him again, go buy the Tina doll and leave her on your back porch at 10:00 today.'

Millie woke up groggy and disorientated on the sofa at four o'clock, with a heavy head. She staggered from the sofa to the hallway, intent on taking a couple of painkillers and getting at least a couple more hours' sleep before Fletcher woke up. On her way past the front door, out of the corner of her eye, she saw a flash of red ribbon. As she turned, she saw it was attached to a large white envelope hanging from the letterbox. She stared, surprised; the posties don't work New Year. She sank onto the bottom of the stairs to open the envelope, far too tired to bother going back into the lounge. Her eyes widened as she read and reread the ransom note. Was this some sort of joke? Millie raced up the stairs to Fletcher's bedroom. He wasn't there; she checked the bathroom, calling his name as she raced from room to room. Panic was taking over now as she flew down the stairs and out of the front door, still in her pyjamas and slippers, to rouse the neighbours for help.

Norman was just on the verge of pouring the milk into his much-deserved cup of tea, feeling quite proud of himself. He was a problem solver, to be sure, when the pounding on the front door made him jump and spill the milk all over the counter. 'Dammit!'

He ran to the door and threw it open before the noise could wake the children to see Millie sobbing on the doorstep, her words barely audible between sobs 'It's Fletcher, he's gone, someone took him, oh god, please help me.'

Norman ushered her into the lounge and as he turned away from her to shut the door, a huge grin lit up his face. He was in his element right now. The only thing better than divorcing this bitch was having her moving in next door so he could mess with her head.

JANUARY SALES

April Berry

Gazing through the window of the local bike shop, I was so excited. I absolutely needed that bike. The beauty of it was astonishing to behold. The paintwork shimmered, the carbon frame was as smooth as a baby's bottom, flexible and light, the equipment was top-notch, smooth gear changes for uphill, hydraulic disc brakes ensured my safety in all weathers.

Apart from an enormous expense for a funeral at the beginning of last year, I'd built up quite a sum of money in my savings account, enough to purchase the bike of my dreams. Was I crazy? I asked myself, spending £5000 on a pushbike. I heard people make remarks like my car didn't cost that. You can get a bike for a tenth of the price. Who in their right mind would pay that much for a pushbike? However, this wasn't just any ordinary push bike, it was the same model that had propelled professional cyclists up Mont Ventoux, glided up La Planche Des Belles Filles to victory in the greatest bike race on earth, and whilst I will never be that winner of the Tour de France, I wanted to ride the best bike I could afford. Also, this bike was generously discounted by 20% in the January sales. Ok, so it was last year's model, but that didn't matter to me, I didn't actually like the new one. I had trawled magazines, done so much research and last years was a better model than this year. Another company that downgraded a product, packaged it as better than last years and charged more. It's amazing what advertising companies can make you believe. They convinced me last year; I had a perfectly good cycle helmet, but the advertising has persuaded me to buy a new one at the beginning of last year. However, to my cost, I discovered it didn't live up to the hype.

The shop door opened. I'd been queuing for what seemed like days, although it was only two hours, two hours of daydreaming about future rides. In the past I had ridden every day, the boring commute, rides by the canal, watching the ducks and swans wandering on the towpath, swerving round them and riding like my life depended on it from the vicious mums protecting their new born cygnets.

I was planning a summer holiday along the Danube, five countries, lots of scenery, exercise excellent food and drinking wine and surveying the scenery in the evening from the boat deck, which would be my floating hotel for ten days.

I ran into the shop, making straight for the bike I had drooled over in magazines for months. It looked spectacular mounted on the podium in the middle of the shop. It surprised me to see only three other people in the shop. I could have sworn the queue behind me was bigger than that.

Winter clothes were another thing I needed. I had lost so much weight last year that none of my existing winter cycling gear fitted me. I made my way over to the clothing section, a guy had stood taking up all the room in front of the jackets, I asked him to move, politely but he just looked straight through me, I tutted, that didn't get any reaction. I reached round him and took a jacket, bib tights and a base layer from the hangers.

I approached the service desk to talk to the customer service assistant about the bike, but they just ignored me, too. No one was taking any notice of me, which made me feel agitated. The money was burning a hole in my pocket; I had dreamed about this bike all year, and my frustration was getting the better of me. I tried to attract the attention of someone who would just let me pay for my stuff and wheel my new pride and joy from the bike showroom.

I turned to the woman behind me in the queue; I needed to vent; I had now been waiting for ten minutes, being ignored by all the people serving in the shop. Suddenly the unthinkable happened, someone walked into the shop, walked up to the guy behind the counter and within 2 minutes was the proud owner of the bike I had craved, dreamed about, drooled over all year.

The woman in the queue behind me tapped me on the arm, don't worry dearie she said, not everyone can see spirits; it's only the chosen few. Momentarily I was shocked, and then the realisation of my predicament hit me. A bit like that transit van did, that was coming around the bend on the wrong side of the road, last Christmas, that I didn't see!

JUST SICK OF IT

Carolyn Ward-Daniels

Kathy was avoiding all the Christmas shoppers and may have literally bumped into her best friend Sal if it hadn't been for the two-metre distancing rule. She smiled affectionately as Sal blew her an air kiss. They would normally have hugged. Kathy pinched the lapels of her coat together to ward off the cold.

'I'll be glad when this covid crap is over. I am absolutely sick of it.'

'I'm struggling to get Christmas presents. There're only supermarkets open and only four weeks to go.'

'I've done all mine,' Sal said smugly. 'I hate the pressure of buying presents. I was sick of that so I bought all mine in the last January sales, wrapped them as well.'

'Oh well done, I've always wanted to do that.'

'I even got your joke pressy too.'

'I can't wait. I still smile at the chocolate penis you got me last year.'

'Well, no chocolate this year. I had to store them in the top of the warm airing cupboard.'

They said their farewells, arranging an outdoor meeting for their ritual of exchanging gifts.

The next two weeks screamed by and Sal asked her husband Ray to get the Christmas tree and decorations from the loft, also the wrapped presents from the airing cupboard. The tree landed first, and she busied herself trimming it. When Ray slid the shiny wrapped parcels from the top shelf, some of the sticky tape had curled in the heat and he pressed them down. A few labels were unattached, but they had settled on parcels, so he stuck them back on. One stuck to his jumper, and he found a parcel without a label and put it right.

It had been a miserable year of lockdowns and this Christmas wouldn't be the same, not being able to have family round. Ray dutifully delivered all the presents, and Kathy and Sal had their distance meeting in the park. They exchanged their joke presents. Sal couldn't help but smirk when she handed over hers. She would love to see Kathy's face on Christmas day when she opened the vibrator disguised as a large lipstick.

Mid Christmas morning, the phone rang. Ray answered it as Sal basted the turkey. She looked puzzled when Ray said his dad loved his cookery book, said he always wanted to experiment with different spices.

'Cookery book? but I bought him a poker game set I think.'

'Oh, Mum is looking forward to having a tot of whiskey in her tea.'

'But I got her bath bombs.'

Sal rang her own mum, who thanked her for the jigsaws. She loved new ones to do 'I hope I didn't get you one you already have and I will miss not having you here for Christmas dinner.'

'I miss you too, but don't worry about dinner, my love. I don't like turkey, sprouts, stuffing or Christmas pudding. My favourite is lasagne, and that's what I'm having.'

Sal resumed her prepping, trying to remember where she had put her present list 11 months ago. Suddenly she dropped everything and rang Kathy.

'Merry Christmas, Sal. I hope you liked your sexy fireman calendar. I love my poker game, a bit sober for you though.'

'Oh my God!'

'I do like it, Sal. Sal.'

'Oh no.'

'I mean it, I've always wanted to learn how to play.'

'Kathy, I'll ring you back later. Merry Christmas.'

In the sideboard drawer, she found the year old present list. She sat down and ran her nail down the paper and spoke to herself as if it would clarify everything. 'Uncle Bill should have had the whiskey. Ray's mum should have had the bath bombs. Aunty Eva should have had the cookery book and Ray's dad should have had the poker game. SHIT!'

Gingerly, she pressed the buttons to phone Uncle Bill and Aunty Eva. 'Hello Uncle Bill, it's Sal, Merry Christmas.'

'Merry Christmas Sal, hey thanks for those bath bombs. It will be lovely to get home from unblocking smelly drains and having a nice soak.'

Sal took a deep breath and said, 'You're welcome, is... is Aunty Eva there?' she closed her eyes and bit her lip.

'She's getting dressed, love, well I think she's getting dressed. She's been upstairs for ages. As soon as she opened your present, off she went. I think she was going to put some makeup on. I'll go shout her.'

'No, no, it's alright I'll catch up with her soon.' Sal found Ray wrist deep in Quality Street seeking his favourites. 'Ray, you know when you delivered the presents, did you get them mixed up?'

'How could I, why?'

'It's just that your dad has got the cookery book I got for Aunty Eva and your mum has got Uncle Bills whiskey.' Ray looked thoughtful as he picked out the toffee penny and then he let out a long 'ooh... ah, I have an idea what might have happened.' Sal's eyebrows rose, her wrinkled brow waiting for the information. Ray was preoccupied, peeling off the bright yellow cellophane.

'What!' She snapped.

'Ah well, when I slid the parcels from the airing cupboard some tags were loose but I guessed they were sitting on the right presents so I secured them back on.'

'Oh my God, Aunty Eva!'

'Is she alright?'

'Well, I think she's having a happy Christmas.'

JUST SICK OF IT

April Berry

Sarah turned to James, an immediate look of disdain crossing her face. James was swigging beer straight from a can, something that Sarah hated and staring inanely at the TV. It wasn't the only thing she hated about James. She couldn't abide the way he loosened his trousers after a meal. He left the toilet seat up, didn't care about the kids. The worst thing though was his hygiene habits, but the less said about that, the better. Sarah tutted loudly, James turned, 'What's up love?' he asked.

'Why can't you have a conversation with me instead of watching that shite all the time?' she snapped at him.

'Precisely because you are always snapping at me, having a go at everything I do and say. So why would you want to talk to me? And anyway, you choose what we watch and it's mind numbing,' James retorted.

Sarah sprang up from the settee and stormed out of the room. Realising she had the TV remote in her hand as she reached the door, turning she threw it at James. It bounced off the side of his head and fell to the floor. Sarah stormed upstairs. She was just sick of all of this.

James smiled to himself, picked up the remote, rapidly flicking through the channels until he found his favourite programme. One he could get lost in, to avoid Sarah's nagging, her constant sniping and complaints about his behaviour. Oh, he knew Sarah was right in lots of ways, but she seemed to overlook her own shortcomings. But James didn't, and it was time to do something about it and teach Sarah a lesson she wouldn't easily forget.

He sat up all night, plotting how he could extricate himself from the situation he found himself in. Ideas taking shape in his head, some ludicrous, some downright stupid. But all concluded with him either killing or leaving Sarah and meeting someone who would appreciate him for him until he finally fell asleep where he sat.

James woke with a jolt. Sarah was looming over him with a thunderous look on her face. She was holding a steaming hot cup of coffee that she thrust at him. James burnt his fingers on the scalding hot mug. Cursing under his breath, he placed the mug on the table at the side of the settee. He pulled his stiff body out of the chair, straightened up slowly, and went upstairs to get ready for work. 'At this rate I'm going to be late!'

Once James arrived at work, he forgot all about Sarah until break time. He was sitting with two of his mates in the canteen discussing the up and coming yearly camping trip to Cornwall that the families went on every year. James mentioned he didn't really want to go this year, explaining to them the state of his marriage and his daydreams of the previous night. Alan, his best friend since primary school, took him to one side as they left the canteen to return to work. Alan had a concerned look on his face. One that worried James a little. Alan started stuttering, something that he only did when he was nervous.

'I had a message from Fiona earlier,' he said to James. Fiona was best friends with Sarah, and in fact always took Sarah's side when she was complaining about James, even took it upon herself to chide James for the way she perceived he treated Sarah sometimes.

'She asked me not to say anything, but Sarah is leaving you and going to stay with her sister for a while until you come to your senses,' Alan said. James stopped listening at that point, elation flooding over him like a wave. He could see Alan talking, but he wasn't listening any longer.

James thought all his Christmases and Birthdays had come at once. He couldn't wait for the end of the working day. Walking home with a spring in his step that he'd not had since the days when he and Sarah first got engaged. He put his key in the lock, turning it with anticipation. Hoping that Fiona wasn't lying. James searched the house, noticed that a lot of Sarah's clothes had gone. Phew, he thought. Grabbing a can of beer from the fridge, he went into the living room to switch on the TV, but searching high and low, he couldn't find the TV remote. He searched in the kitchen, bedroom, spare room.

His phone pinged. It was a WhatsApp picture from Sarah of the TV remote. James stood in the middle of the room, she could even piss him off when she wasn't in the same place as him, but his anger turned to disbelief when he realised that without the remote he couldn't watch his hero on the television tonight, the first time he had ever missed an episode of Karl Pilkington 'Sick of it.'

JUST SICK OF IT

Daizi Rae

Millie sat nursing a glass of wine, with her usual tears and despondency, trying her damnedest to remember what she had ever seen in Norman and finding nothing. He'd pretty much always been a sanctimonious son of a bitch. Belittling her as a wife, and more recently, undermining her as a mother. Over the years she'd argued with him, screamed at him, pleaded with him, tried to appeal to the better man that she imagined must hide inside him somewhere, but all to no avail. The more wine she drank, the more bitter she became. The more bitter she was, the more she just wanted to bury an ice pick in his skull to look a little deeper for the 'good!#in Norman. But no, he was at his happiest when Millie was in tears, and here she was again, in tears. He'd love to see her like this. Well, never again. She was just sick of it. She'd show him!

Millie planned to surprise the hell out of him and show him she was a better woman than he'd ever given her credit for. She secretly hired a landscaper to redesign Norman's gardens, building a new summerhouse where the dilapidated shed had stood, with a cute little hot tub and a minibar. A gorgeous patio area outside the kitchen door, with seating, luscious plants and a BBQ, he'd always loved a BBQ had Norman, showing off his cooking prowess to the neighbours, not that she'd ever been that impressed, but it made him happy. Oh, and she'd even included a treehouse for the kids with a swing hanging off one branch. They'd love that, having their friends round and hanging out in their own space as they got older.

Having a project was the making of Millie. She felt motivated to get up in the mornings, excited with all her plans. Overjoyed at keeping it all secret from Norman, for now. Clandestine meetings with the landscaper while Norman was at work and the kids were at school. This was going to be the making of her broken little family. She just knew it.

The highlight of controlling and punishing Millie for being so weak and pathetic, for Norman, was when he rented the little house next door and made Millie move out of the family home.

It was heartbreaking for her. Norman made sure of it. He fought her on every single thing. She couldn't take any furniture with her, not even pots and pans, and most of her wardrobe mysteriously vanished when she went to pack her clothes. He made sure she'd go alone with nothing, not even the kids. He would stay in their home that they built tougher, and he would keep the children, and leave her to sit alone right next door in her grotty rental watching Norman and her children having a wonderful time without her. Norman was at his absolute happiest when he was in control. Control was everything.

Millie had spent months fighting through the courts, trying to get custody of her children. Despite Norman being a master at undermining her at every opportunity, Millie did eventually get custody of their youngest child, Fletcher, but not her daughter. It devastated her. The judge decided the children would still have a close relationship and suffer no detriment, as they would live next door to one another. Norman had broken her. Job well done, Norman!

Operation Garden, as Millie had taken to calling it, was going great. She enlisted the help of the next door but one neighbour, Jenny. A splendid choice, as Jenny knew everyone on the street and loved a secret even more than she loved her pampered pooch Percy. Jenny was old school and believed in marriage for life, no matter what a husband might get up to.

Millie hinted at her worries that Norman may have met someone else, but she wanted to save her marriage before it was too late. She just knew Jenny was the perfect person to help her fix her marriage, so she confided in her that very morning that Norman was off on a business trip today, for the rest of the week, until Friday. The excavator would arrive to demolish the old shed and dig the foundations for the summerhouse. And if Jenny wouldn't mind, could she pick the kids up from school while Millie set the team of landscapers to building the new patio? And didn't she think it would thrill Norman when he came home on Friday evening.

The workmen had finished by Wednesday teatime. The early finish cash bonus was a great incentive to do a perfect and super-efficient job. Millie invited Jenny over to see the finished garden and they giggled like schoolgirls over how impressed with Millie Norman would be on Friday when he got home. This was going to be a fabulous new start to the marriage, and the family will be back all under one roof in no time. Norman was going to love that summerhouse with its new hot tub and bar. Millie said he'd never be out of it. Jenny agreed. She was so happy to see Millie, so enthusiastic and excited about Norman's return. She'd been so worried about Millie until now.

When Jenny went home, Millie stayed at Normans. She put the kids to bed, poured herself a glass of wine, and went and sat out on the patio. All of her family under one roof, with no more problems. She raised her glass to the summerhouse.

'Cheers Norman, I don't need to dig too deep to find the best of you now, do I.'

Jenny would be so disappointed for Millie when Norman didn't come home on Friday.

IT'S COMPLICATED

Elaine Morris

Just one more row.

Isn't the English language amazing? If you didn't know what the person was thinking, you wouldn't be able to build a mental image of the activity. Is it a queue or a quarrel? A line on a spreadsheet or the action of moving a boat with oars? Or, maybe, a consecutive sequence of similar actions, like crochet or knitting?

Here it's knitting! Despite the visual complexity of completed knitted garments, toys and household objects, particularly to the uninitiated, there are only two stitches; to be repeated in sequential actions, row after row. Within a relationship, the craft may lead to quarrels 'Not more wool!' and serious knitters will create queues of the next projects to be completed. Indeed, crafters have their own world of U.F.O's, UnFinished Objects.

Life was complicated indeed; a constant pressure, the requirement to prioritise the needs and expectations of others above one's own. Individuals could be so demanding (and unreasonable), organisations so distant and disconnected, never considering the fact that there were conflicting priorities in the world. Instead of the knitting that should be front and centre of anyone's 'To Do' list, there were other tasks to be considered; cooking, cleaning, ironing (oh, those dreaded shirts). If we could eliminate those tasks, then concentration could be given to the needles and being able to use them to create something beautiful and useful.

What it needed was a plan, how to eliminate the complications of life. There was pleasure and satisfaction to be had in using elements of the craft in the plan. So, carry on knitting: smooth, rhythmic, repetitive actions allowed the mind to wander; to concentrate and drift at the same time. A plan formed before the mind's eye, much as an Aran pattern forms from the manipulation of stitches on the needle.

A needle was required, a very long, extremely sharp needle. It had to be steel, to allow it to be boiled and cleansed, leaving no trace of the victim or perpetrator. It had to be fine, so its insertion point might be overlooked, and it had to be long enough to inflict the necessary damage. The trick was to insert the needle, just like in a single stitch, just like a single point in a timeline, to such a depth that the heart damages itself against the point, repeatedly, rhythmically.

Of course, for now at least, this was only spinning a yarn, another distraction to get through the long, long days. It was comforting enough for now to have a plan; the target was available; the tools were to hand, the opportunity would come.

And then, the relentless, unceasing motion of the heart would cease, life would have its own pattern, the twists and turns of the complicated relationship would be over and all trivial distractions eliminated, leaving only the important task of creativity through knitting.

There was the familiar sound of the key in the lock. Life was about to go on the same and maybe take an unexpected turn.

Who could tell? Ah well, just another row.

IT'S COMPLICATED

Daizi Rae

Jenny feels so much love and longing welling up inside herself, she's sure it must be obvious to anyone that looks at her. Someone will notice, surely. To see it, to hear it, to call her out on it. How can she feel this deeply and no one else sees it? At any moment, her lover, Amanda, will look at her face, and her cover will be blown, and there it will be, larger than life, impossible to deny. But no! The days turn into weeks, turn into months, turn into years, and no one, not even Amanda, really sees Jenny, despite the daily dutiful 'love you, baby.'

Jenny sits at the dressing table, watching all this hidden emotion behind her own eyes in the mirror. She closes her eyes against it, but Macy's face, as always, is right there. Those intense blue eyes staring right at her in that direct way she has. If only she dare gaze right back and speak the truth. Macy is the last thing Jenny thinks of every night before she falls asleep, her first thought every morning. Every blessed daydream, which gets no further than the perfect image of Macy standing in front of her, placing one hand on Jenny's waist, and pulling her in close, close enough for their lips to touch for that first blissful kiss.

What's that about anyway, who spends four years daydreaming about a first kiss? It's a little weird, right? Not realistic, that's for sure. And talking of not realistic, Jenny picks up the hairspray, contemplating it thoughtfully. Accidents happen in the home all the time. It wouldn't be the first time a faulty aerosol exploded. She thought about how steep their stairs were and how easily one could slip on that shiny wooden floor. Amanda listens to the radio all the time in the bathroom. Now that's an accident waiting to happen.

Jenny sighed, Daydreams don't make your morning brew, or set three alarms to make sure you get your lazy arse out of bed for work of a morning. Daydreams don't let the dog out for a morning wee before they both come through to snuggle on the bed for a morning cuppa before the day starts. But daydreams also don't have you live on the outskirts of their life, a permanent guest without a home.

She padded through to the kitchen where Amanda had just returned from a dawn shopping trip to the supermarket to avoid other people. That was the norm now. She was busy cleaning the latest batch of shopping before putting it away, just to be safe. 'Morning baby, do you want a cuppa to take upstairs to work with you?' She asked Jenny.

'yes please, that'd be lovely,' Jenny smiled as she kissed Amanda on the cheek on her way to the toaster.

Jenny kissed Amanda one last time on her way out of the kitchen with her tea and toast and told her, 'have a good morning, I'll see you at lunchtime, love ya.'

'Ok, love you too.' They smiled at one another and blew each other an air kiss as they parted.

As she reached the top step, Jenny's foot slid out from under her and she could feel herself losing her balance. Instinct made her let go of the tea and toast and grab for the banister to save herself, to no avail. Maybe the abandoned tea had made her hand too wet to grip it. Both Jenny and her breakfast hit the stairs just once on the way down, shattering her spine and the plate on impact. Jenny landed unconscious on the hallway floor on her broken back, swiftly followed by shards of crockery, which sliced the length of her cheek before landing on the floor beside her.

As her eyes fluttered open, she saw Amanda kneeling beside her, looking shocked and scared. 'Oh god, Jenny, I heard the noise from the kitchen. Are you ok, can you move?' She saw a tear slide down her lover's cheek as she gently took Jenny's mobile phone and slid it across the hallway floor until it was out of sight behind the Yukka plant. Amanda stood up, and as she backed away, tears streaming down her face, she whispered, 'I do love you Jenny, but it's complicated.'

IT'S COMPLICATED

April Berry

'It's complicated,' said Bruce, running his hands through his hair in exasperation.

'It always is with you.' Lucy was losing the will to live, trying to negotiate with Bruce. 'tell me why this time?'

Bruce looked at the floor, wondering which of the half dozen reasons would work best with Lucy. Whilst Lucy was waiting for him to respond, she was thinking about all the times over the last twelve months that Bruce had objected to when she wanted to do anything or go anywhere, whether it was with or without him. Finally, Bruce just trotted out the same ludicrous excuses as he had dozens of times before, who would pick the children up from school, who would look after them when he had football practice, drinks on the way home from work with his mates. The weekend cycle rides with the club he belonged to. All the household chores that would be neglected whilst she was away. Bruce then turned on his heel before Lucy had any chance to counteract the excuses.

Lucy sighed and picked up the phone. After a fifteen-minute call with her mother, she shouted up stairs 'all sorted' she said 'my mum is going to stay here whilst I am away.' Bruce knew he was beat on the domestic front, so would have to find another, more substantial reason Lucy couldn't go away for two weeks. Lucy smiled to herself, knowing that over the next month Bruce would find as many obstacles as he could for her not to go. Lucy couldn't really pinpoint the exact date when Bruce had turned into a possessive husband. He was always so easygoing and was the first to accept invitations to parties, events, concerts, but gradually, that had changed. Maybe it was the new job, thought Lucy, vowing to have a heart to heart conversation before she went away to understand the change in him.

Lucy was looking forward to the trip. It was one she had volunteered for two years ago but had only made the waiting list. It was the trip of a lifetime, though she knew it would also bring its hardships. Counting penguins in the Antarctic would be cold, with temperatures as low as minus 55 degrees. However, as a zoologist at the local wildlife park, Lucy knew that research expeditions didn't come along very often. Penguins were Lucy's favourite animals, and the opportunity to see them in their natural habitat was the chance of a lifetime, one she would not pass up just so Bruce could go to the pub with his mate on a Friday night and cycle round the countryside in Lycra frightening the population at weekends.

Then Bruce had a change of heart. Apologised for being an ass and re-assured Lucy that everything would be just fine. Lucy made preparations, buying the clothes from the recommended list and extra equipment, which would help combat the freezing conditions and the fact that for the whole three weeks she would be away, it wouldn't be daylight once. Even so, the excitement kept bubbling away inside her.

She showed the children where she'd be staying, as this would be the first time that she would be away from them for this length of time, reassuring them she would ring and speak to them as often as she could.

Lucy mentally made a list of questions to ask at the briefing session so the group could get to know each other before the trip. The group comprised zoologists from around the country, two professors and three students from the local University, who were part funding the trip.

On the evening of the briefing which was being held at the library in town, there was a presentation from the University, a schedule of the trip, it's aims and what they were hoping to achieve. Also a chance to ask questions and have a tour of the research station via a video link with some researchers already at the station, who would look after the group whilst they were in the Antarctic. Lucy looked round the room. The students looked so young, and she vowed to help them as much as possible. After all, they were not much older than her son Luke, who had just turned fifteen.

The group retired to the pub across the street from the library and were talking about their families, what their own personal goals were regarding the trip, hopes and dreams, as what possibilities the trip would open up for them. One voice stood out over all the rest. The student was talking about being away from her fiancée for three weeks, how she was going to cope, and that once she got back, they were going to plan the wedding. Melanie was extolling his virtues and how kind, caring, and loving he was and how gorgeous he was. Lucy was phasing off into a world of her own. Young love, she thought, how sweet. Do you want to see a photo of him, asked Melanie and before anyone could answer, giggling, Melanie, opened her phone and showed the group a picture of Bruce.

Lucy drained her glass, bid farewell to the group and went home to have the heart to heart she had promised herself last week that she would have with her husband.

COME ON, OPEN THE DOOR

TJ Spencer & Dean Wrigley

Last two deliveries of the day. One of mine. One of the missus. Just gotta find this address, deliver this parcel, knock off and get myself back home in time. It's the second kid and we're having it at home. Where's that address? 29c Rothsey Avenue. The posh side of town. La-di-dah, more money than sense types.

Dingalingaling.

Dingalingaling.

Dingalingaling.

Ooh, the missus calling. What's she want?

Dingalingaling.

Dingalingaling.

Dingalingaling.

'Hi love, what's up?'

He listens…. 'Your waters, oh heck! What's that, your Karen's taking you to hospital, ok, well I'll see you there. Won't be long, just one more delivery. Gotta go, boss doesn't like calls while I'm working. Yeah, I know. Yeah, see ya in a bit, love you. Bye. Bye. Bye.'

He hangs up.

Right, what's that address? 17, 19, erm, erm, 23, 27, 31, 33. Eh? I've missed it. How did that happen? Ah, stuff this. Park up here and walk. 33, 31… 27 Eh? Where the? Ah! Well, that's mad. 29 is behind 27.

Dingalingaling.

Dingalingaling.

Dingalingaling.

Yes, yes, one moment babe. Ok, 29… C? 29c? Where's that?

'Hey up, love, what's up? Oh hi Karen, her bag for the hospital? It's in the bedroom. Ok, see ya at the hospital. Drive careful. Laters.'

Right now 29c, ah, here we go. Oh, a flat. Best ring that bell. He presses doorbell marked 29c. It rings, again it rings. No answer. He rings again. *Come on, come on, open up, open the door…* He waits, rings the doorbell again. The door swings open.

'You Mr.. Oh sorry are you Mrs. Cross?'

'No love, but I know you.'

'Don't think so!'

'It's Craig, isn't it? Craig Ashton.'

'Uh yeah, that's right. Do I know you?'

'It's Tania, Tania Cross. Remember?'

'No, sorry. Uh, I have a parcel for Mr. Cross.'

He's cut short by the woman. 'My name's Tania. You remember me, don't ya?'

'Tania, oh yeah, yeah, course. Look, Tania, I gotta deliver this.'

'Ok, so where have you been hiding?'

'Hiding, not me, I've been getting on with my life.'

'Oh yeah, what's that mean.'

'I got married, second kid on the way now!'

'Second! You've been busy.'

'Yeah, and I must deliver this, then I gotta get to hospital.'

'Oh, right? In a rush, are you?'

'Something like that.'

'Well, before you go, you best come up.'

'No time. Can you just sign for the parcel please?'

'In a minute, come up just for a minute.'

'I can't, sorry.'

'Just for a minute.'

'Can't, gotta go.'

'Look Craig, this will take a minute.'

'If I do, will you take the parcel?'

'Yeah, yeah, of course.'

Craig follows Tania up the stairs, clinging onto the parcel. She opens a door, it's marked 29c. 'Come on in. Lia?'

'Lia, who's Lia?'

'Mummy, is it here?'

'Yes, darling.'

A little blonde girl waddles into the hallway of the flat. 'Oh hello, who are you?' Tania turns to the girl. Bending over, she touches the girl's arm.

'I have a surprise for you.'

'A surprise, oh is it my parcel?' The child smiles excitedly.

'Well, yes, but I have a bigger surprise.' Suddenly Craig's mobile rings again.

Dingalingaling.

Dingalingaling.

Dingalingaling.

'Can I just drop this parcel off, I gotta go.' Craig grows anxious.

'In a mo. Look Craig, it's like this.'

'What? Like what? I gotta go. My missus is about to have our child and…'

'And this is Lia, your daughter!'

Craig's jaw drops open.

'Say what?'

'Lia, this is your daddy, Craig.'

The little girl jumps up and down with glee. 'Daddy!'

'What's going on here? You're crazy.'

'Crazy, you think I'm crazy?'

Tania sidles up to Craig. 'I wasn't crazy when you gave me that other package five years ago, was I?'

Dingalingaling.

Dingalingaling.

Dingalingaling.

COME ON, OPEN THE DOOR

Carolyn Ward-Daniels

It was promising to be a nice day, even at 6am. Robert Arby was delivering milk. He didn't mind the early starts, preferred them, in fact; as there weren't many people around and he didn't much care for other people. He was also home for lunchtime. He would have a chip shop lunch and doss on the couch in front of the TV for the rest of the day or read his Marvel comics. At 35, this was his only reading matter.

Sometimes he would venture out to get a kebab or pizza, but mostly his dinner was crisp sandwiches and chocolate. He didn't drink alcohol as he quickly got out of control; it didn't mix well with his medication.

He was on his last delivery and just as he placed 2 bottles of milk on the steps of a posh town house; the door opened and startled him. His chunky body shuffled backwards, and his round face looked a little shocked as the most beautiful woman stepped out. She saw his blushed face, smiled at him as she swept her dark hair away from her pale amber eyes. A taxi pulled up, and she hurried toward it. Robert couldn't take his eyes off her. He drove the milk float back in a daze, as he couldn't get her out of his mind. He was sure he knew her.

His everyday pattern took him to the chip shop, then his untidy flat where he made a pot of tea, the only cooking he ever did. He took his food to the lounge and turned on the TV. Eating straight out of the styrene carton, he was just about to deliver the last chip to his open mouth when the 1 o'clock news came on.

There she was, his beautiful woman reading the news. Now he knew her name, knew where she worked and knew where she lived. The chip never got delivered but dropped in the carton, which dropped on the floor with the other debris of pizza boxes and chocolate bar wrappers. He got mad when the camera left her face to show a newsreel and felt peculiar and nice when her face came back on and she was looking at him and talking
to him. He felt quite bereft when she was saying goodbye until she said, 'until later with the news at six.' She was coming

back; he looked around and realised it was messy, so he collected all the rubbish off the floor and binned it. He washed his dirty mug and teaspoon that had a dross of brown tea crusted in the bowl as he just used it repeatedly without a clean.

He didn't know what to do with himself until 6 o'clock, couldn't even concentrate on his Hulk comic. He changed his clothes, putting on a shirt with a collar, combed his greasy brown hair at 5 to 6 and sat down, excited when the jingle for the news piped up. Then a bloke filled the screen, a serious faced, grey-haired bloke.

'No! No...Where is she? Get off you!' Robert wasn't listening to the news, he was angry, 'GET OFF! GET OFF! GET OFF!' he shouted at the screen. He was striding to and from the TV, constantly clicking his fingers and cursing. It had been ages since he had a temper episode and he went to his goody drawer, took out three chocolate bars and took them to bed. The following day as he approached her door, milk in hand, he was whispering, 'Come on, open the door,' but it didn't. He was ready in front of the TV for 1 o'clock, and there she was. He was hoping for good news as when she smiled, his heart melted. He now knelt in front of the TV screen and when she said goodbye, he kissed her on screen and a buzz of static made him realise she had kissed him back.

Day after day, he watched and listened, but what Robert heard was different. Out of Robert Mugabe, he heard his name: Robert Arby. He picked out random words that he wanted to hear. 'I will see you later at 6 Robert.' The messages got stronger, from the announcement about the bumper crop of best dates from the Middle East. Robert heard, 'We will have the best date this year.' He could have sworn she winked at him and when he kissed the screen he heard her say, 'see you later,' he knew he had a date.

He got busy ironing his only decent pair of trousers, had a shower and shaved. Bought flowers on his way to his date and caught a bus that would get him there before six. He knew there was a bus stop at the end of her road, just after the railway bridge. It was a quarter to six when he got off the bus and he was trembling with nerves. He leant on the brick wall overlooking the railway tracks and counted to 100 to calm himself down. Then he started down the street toward her house, his heart banging in his rib cage, and then he got a massive blushing attack when he saw her walking down the pavement toward him. They were both four houses away from her gate when a taxi pulled up. A smart chap got out. She broke into that beautiful smile and in a few brief steps, they were embracing before going down the path and into the house.

Robert froze and dropped the flowers. He backtracked to the railway bridge, clicking his fingers in time to his fast stride. He knew how to make her face sad about losing him, and have his name on her lips on the news tomorrow, as he hurled himself over the railway bridge into the path of the oncoming train.

COME ON, OPEN THE DOOR

Gerry O'Keeffe

'Have you got it, Frankie?'

'No! I've tried everywhere.'

'Everywhere?'

'Yes, everywhere!'

'The all night petrol station?'

'The first place I went. Come on, open the door, Sammy. It's freezing out here, and it's 3am in the morning.'

'No! You promised, and I'm in a lot of pain here. I need it.'

'I know, sweetheart, but everyone is looking for some. There are a lot of others in your condition at the moment, and the freak weather has destroyed nearly every plant or field that grows it or provides the ingredients to make it.'

'You don't love me. I'm too fat, aren't I? You're punishing me, aren't you?'

'No, honestly I'm not. Now please let me in. My fingers are going numb. I've driven to every late night shop, pharmacy, you name it, I've been there. I just can't find any. Look at me! Cut's and bruises all over my face and hands. Some old lady beat me up and stabbed me with her knitting needles to get to some. There are fights breaking out everywhere. It's bedlam out here.' The letterbox opened on the door of the semi-detached house where all this raucous shouting was going on. Two beady eyes look out to survey the scene outside.

'Oh, sweetheart, you look terrible, but you're not coming in. I need some baby. I'm hurting so much!'

They pushed an envelope with a wad of cash and instructions through the letterbox.

'Here's the address of a supplier, plus some extra cash to complete the transaction.'

'Where did you get this money? And how do you know about this supplier?'

'You don't need to know, and it's better that way.'

'OK! OK! I'll be back in about half an hour and you better be right.' The car door slams and their car leaves the driveway.

'Sammy better be right, and I will not be messing about' Taking a gun out of the glove compartment, Frankie lays it on the passenger seat. It was snowing heavily now, and visibility was bad. Frankie was struggling to see and cursing Sammy for this terrible night. Frankie soon found the right place. There was an underpass of an old railway crossing with what looked like an old air raid shelter underneath. 'This looks like the place.' Gun safely stashed out of sight in a back pocket, Frankie got out of the car and walked over to the shelter and knocked on the door, which caused pain to shoot through Frankie's frostbitten hand. Cursing, Frankie watched as the door slowly opened to reveal an older woman, in a woolly hat and scarf, wearing a long black trench coat, holding bloodied knitting needles. Frankie's heart sank. She dropped a salacious wink and asked, 'Are you looking for these?' As she opened her coat to reveal pocket after pocket with various packets and boxes of almost any kind you could wish for.

'I'll take the lot.'

'It'll cost you. Have you got the money?'

Frankie replied, 'I think this will cover it,' handing over the envelope. The woman flicked through the wad of cash, sniffing it joyfully, then said, smiling.

'That will do nicely.' She threw everything into a plastic bag and handed it over. Meanwhile, Sammy was sitting on the sofa of their middle-class suburban home, waiting for Frankie to return, getting increasingly agitated and muttering, 'I need some desperately to take away this pain. It has been over an hour now. Where is Frankie!' Suddenly there was a knock at the door, and Sammy ran excitedly to kneel at the letter letterbox to ask. 'Do you have it?'

'Yes!' was the reply, along with a sample posted through the letterbox. 'Now come on, open the door.'

'Oh Darling. This is wonderful.' Sammy opened the door and threw his arms around his lovely wife, Frankie.

She said, 'Don't squeeze too hard. You might hurt the baby. I'm so glad you get to carry this one. This craving, though, it'll be the death of me. I wasn't this bad when I had our first. It was only peanut butter and pickled onions with celery. Getting hold of this chocolate is much harder. I hope you appreciate that Old

Jamaican Rum and Raisin. That is priceless now, it's so hard to get hold of.'

Frankie handed over the rest of the bag, which included Jaffa cakes, red bounties, and Thorntons selection boxes, Chocolate Digestives, Viscounts, Penguins and a Terry's Chocolate Orange. 'That's Frankie's not Terry's.' She grinned, grabbing back the already half-eaten box. 'But that lot should keep you going for a while.' She grinned. Sammy grinned back mischievously. 'Oh sweetheart, I'm sorry I put you through all this, just getting my own back for when you were having Ben. What do you think we'll have this time?'

'Must be a girl, especially wanting all this chocolate.'

'Oi cheeky!' Slapping Frankie playfully over the head, while cramming in a bit more of the old Jamaican Rum and Raisin. They hugged and started laughing.

'Possibly!' they said together.

COME ON, OPEN THE DOOR

Daizi Rae

I like to imagine that there are doors that allow us to wander between worlds, but if I were to take that a step further and imagine my mind was a world, what then. Could you just let yourself in and explore all the things I've done, right or wrong, the things I'm proud or ashamed of. Lift up the edges of the carpets and let out all that has been swept under there?

I imagine you waking up in your own bedroom one morning soon, to find a mysterious door hanging in midair, right in front of you. A literal door, hanging right there in mid-air, no frame to hold it up. You're still a bit sleep fazed, but you stand up to look at it more closely and as you walk around it you realise it vanishes as you walk behind it. It's only visible from the front. You're standing back in front of the door with a decision to make. Either it's part of your dream, so you can get back into bed and forget it, or it's real and you want to see what happens if you try to open the door.

You give yourself a bit of a mental shake and dare yourself 'come on, open the door' and you do... you walk boldly through it into my mind. The other woman.

How much it will hurt you to see our courtship, the romance, the laughter, how we got to know one another. Conversations right through the night, secrets shared, stories told. The fresh flowers we picked on our walk through the park, the feel of her hand protective on the small of my back as we crossed the road.

You can see the funny little post-it notes I find in all kinds of cute places. You watch our first kiss and see our relationship growing from strength to strength; see my memories of shared love making whenever we got the chance, the way she tenderly washed me in the shower afterwards, only for us to make love again while we were in there. You can watch me falling in love with the woman of my dreams.

I know with full certainty in my heart how much this will hurt you if you step through that door, because it is hurting me now.

You see, I got a glimpse into my lover's mind this morning, and I found you in there, a woman she loves, despite being in my bed. I am heartbroken to find you there and to know that you're her wife. You're the loyal, funny, intelligent, beautiful woman that walks in her mind when she sleeps, as you walk beside her every day.

This morning she sat across the table at breakfast looking at me like I was the only woman in the world, and for the first time since I met her, I saw the lie.

She kissed me goodbye on her way out the door without seeing the hurt in my eyes or the barely concealed tears I struggled to keep inside, and I realised she doesn't see me at all. You could, if you looked hard enough, see all of that, without the aid of a door between our minds. So I will call your wife today to tell her I won't see her anymore. I'm truly sorry.

LOCKED

Dean Wrigley

I pulled up a chair to the window, tucked the skirt of my dress under my thighs and settled down to watch the strange-looking bird as it wandered across the patchy, snow-covered lawn. I had seen its brown plumage first and had wondered what a duck was doing in my garden, but when it turned its head towards me, it was obviously not a duck. Whatever it was, it wasn't supposed to be here. I reached for my Illustrated Guide to British Birds.

I slowly thumbed through the pages, keeping an eye on the bird. This bird had a distinctive long beak that it kept pushing into the thawing ground, pulling it out slightly now and then so it could gobble up the insect larva it had caught.

I settled on a page. The drawing on the page looked very similar to the bird on my lawn - the beak was long and the plumage an exact match. I identified it as being a woodcock. The description said it lives in woods and copses and is nocturnal. Well, that didn't make any sense, as it was in my garden at 10 o'clock in the morning! That bird isn't supposed to be here.

I sipped my coffee and contemplated what had brought it here. The weather had been freezing for the past week and perhaps my lawn was the nearest place it could find where it could forage for a meal. The book said it has a call of 'zwick,' but it made no mention of it having a fear of cats. It would need one if it hung around here for much longer. It wasn't supposed to be here.

It wasn't supposed to be here - a bit like me, really.

There are parts of me that have never belonged and for too many years, I hid it all inside. Now I see people pointing and I hear them laughing at this ridiculous clown dressed in his pinks and purples, with a flamboyant air, more Grayson Perry than of the dowdy old widower I'm supposed to be, but I refuse to be bullied and pigeonholed. I'm happy now, being the person I always wanted to be. Too long in the tooth to remain locked into a life I never asked for.

It was twenty years ago that my darling wife finally succumbed to the cancer that had ravaged through her body. During her final years, there was little time for my selfish gender identity trials. The final diagnosis that her cancer was terminal hit me hardest, realising I would be the one left behind. She needed someone to be brave with her, but I knew I had always been a coward. At sixty years old, my whole life had been a lie. I was not supposed to be here.

To me, fatherhood was just motherhood by a different name, and it came easily to me. With the birth of our third child, I questioned my wife about how I had fathered three children. She smiled and simply said, 'Love found a way.' Our daughter brought me particular pleasure as I threw myself into dressing her in the frilly dresses I had adored so much as a confused child. When my eldest son was on the way, my parents were thrilled and grateful they were finally getting the grandchild they had longed for. Unfortunately, neither of my parents got to meet him.

Despite my libido difficulties, my wife and I adored each other. She would make summer dresses with elasticised waistbands that looked really pretty when viewed in the full-length mirror in our bedroom. She made me feel so special. With her, I was where I belonged.

We had exchanged rings to the refrain of The Beatles' song 'You've Got to Hide Your Love Away.' She was the first girl I had dated, much to everyone's surprise. It was 1965.

Even though I flourished in my trade, I found it difficult to make friends. I had nothing in common with any of my male colleagues, most of my female colleagues just saw me as being a nice boy, and that I wasn't interested in them.

I had been apprenticed and employed as a journalist for the local newspaper after my graduation, which followed three years of solid study and virtually no social life.

Throughout my confused adolescence, I fought desperately hard with so many gender demons. The discovery of any sort of sexual desire went unfulfilled. Enrolment into The Boy Scouts didn't bring the male bonding my parents had hoped for and the boxing gloves Santa had brought to toughen me up lay unused in a box in the attic. I wasn't meant to be here.

I was the child who dressed the dollies, always jealous they were dressed in the clothes I wanted to wear. I was meant to be a girl. I have always been a girl.

However, the boy's body I was locked into was all the world wanted me to be.

LOCKED

April Berry

Will was prodding the screen of his phone maniacally, trying and failing to unlock it, beaten again. He sighed and threw his phone on the settee in frustration, running his hands through his hair, as if that would give him the inspiration he needed. In reality, the only thing running through his mind was last night, clouding his thought process, fighting with his hangover for headspace. He rose from the settee and wandered through to the kitchen. Maybe a sandwich and a cuppa would help.

As he gathered the ingredients for his sandwich, his mind still stuck on last night, he reminisced. He hadn't danced or laughed so much for a long time. Had he dreamt it? He hoped not. Alcohol had an uncanny knack of robbing precious memories. It wasn't often Will actually went out, but he'd finished the latest game on his Xbox, so when he was invited on an impromptu Friday night out with his colleagues, he didn't really have a reason to say no. So he said yes.

He remembered the meal in the pub; he was self-conscious about eating with strangers, but he'd overcome that by using a distraction suggested by an old colleague; imagine everyone naked, or sat on the loo. Will thought the loo thing was maybe a step too far, though, not ideal in a dinner situation. He also remembered talking to a friendly guy at the bar when he was ordering his meal. Talking to strangers was something completely out of the ordinary for him, as shy as he was. He bumped into the same guy, Liam, at the next pub, and again they chatted as Will became more confident with every drink.

Will invited Liam to tag along with them as they moved from bar to bar. This was a strange situation for him. He normally didn't have time for many people. Oh, he liked the people he worked with well enough, even Bill in accounts, who had a strange habit of snorting after what he thought was a humorous statement, and Linda in HR, who was always stopping by his desk. He knew she had more than a passing interest in him. She wasn't really his type, though. Not that Will didn't like women, just not as a partner.

Still plagued with some gaps in his memory, Will finished making his sandwich, wiped down the kitchen surfaces, and took his snack back into the living room. He dropped onto the settee, promptly sitting on the phone he had abandoned earlier. He pulled it out from under his backside and switched his attention to the screen as he absentmindedly ate his sandwich.

Wills frustration was turning into desperation, as he stabbed at the screen of his phone frantically. 'You stupid idiot,' he exclaimed out loud 'why did you do that?' He was getting more frantic as every second passed. He'd promised Liam he'd call him today!

His ring tone, Sweet but psycho, made him jump as it started up at far too high a volume. Quite apt really, just about summed up Will's state of mind right now. He stopped breathing for a moment as he saw Liam's name pop up on the screen. He nervously swiped the screen to answer the phone, and while he tried to think of how to start the conversation, he heard Liam's voice say 'Hi Will, I hope you didn't mind me ringing you?'

'Of course not' said Will, as relief washed over him, 'I'm so glad you did. I tried to ring you earlier, but I drunkenly changed my passcode on my phone last night. I still can't remember what I changed it to, so it's locked until my memory comes back. I'm so sorry.'

Liam burst out laughing 'You changed it to my name, he giggled, 5426.'

LOCKED

Daizi Rae

Marina took in a deep breath and held back the tears long enough to pack a suitcase again, for the third time in as many months. She was going to visit her mum for a few days while Ruby took some time out to sort out what it is she really wanted from their relationship. They seemed to be locked into this pattern of needing a break; it was always at the end of the month, and each time it made Marina a little more insecure. It dented her self-esteem and created a long weekend of comfort eating, binge drinking and the consequential self-loathing that inevitably followed.

The first time it happened, it devastated her. She had thought they were so happy, but around a week before Ruby asked her to leave for a few days, she had found fault with things, stupid stuff really, like the way Marina dressed, little digs about her weight, or the people she talked to. Ruby moved into the spare room and Marina could hear muffled phone conversations late into the night. However, if she asked about them, Ruby was adamant she'd just been thinking aloud.

That first time, when Ruby eventually called to say Marina could come back home, she was so relieved. Whatever Ruby needed to work through was over, so she just accepted it, went home, and let it go.

When it happened again the following month, Marina wanted to talk about it when she went home. Talk about what the issues were and see if they couldn't work through them and resolve them, to strengthen their relationship. It made her sad to think that Ruby was so unhappy that she had needed to be alone, and it forced Marina to leave her home, twice. But Ruby wrapped her arms around her, kissed her gently and assured her it wasn't necessary and they were just fine now. So Marina let it go. She wanted to believe her.

If only that had been the case. The third time it happened, Marina was a lot less inclined to leave. She dug her heels in and told Ruby she loved her, and surely, they could talk this out together. Didn't they love one another enough to be open and honest in the name of saving their relationship? Ruby warned her that if she insisted on pushing her, it would turn into a row and they might not come back from that. Marina tried one more time, regardless. Ruby turned on her and spat, 'maybe I'd love you more if you weren't so fat. Now leave it alone and go to your mothers!' Marina was stunned. The attack left her speechless, and she left without another word. When the call came a few days later for Marina to go home, unlike previous times, there was no whoop of joy. She didn't rush out the door to go home. Instead, her mum gently asked her, 'are you sure you want to go back Marina? You seem so unhappy and don't think I haven't noticed that you've barely touched any food the whole time you've been here. I love you darling, I just want you to be happy.'

'I know you do mum, I love you too, but I have to try.' Marina and her mum hugged one another, and Marina left to go home.

Marina sat in her car on the way home wishing emotional breakdowns burned calories and her tears were actually just little globules of fat running out of her eyes to be gone forever. She could cry herself thin and desirable. She had been locked into this cycle of perpetual fatness and loveless misery for months now. No wonder Ruby struggled so much to love her. Just then, Clive's name popped up on her mobile phone, and Marina smiled to see her best friend was calling her. She was always happy to be distracted by him, so she hit the answer button and his voice floated through the car stereo on hands free. 'Hello you gorgeous creature you, I thought I'd call you and check up on you.'

Marina laughed despite herself. 'Hi yourself, what you up to?' 'Well, I've just left yours, actually. I thought I'd bring round that Stephen King book you want to borrow. But that was just an excuse to come over for a gossip really, it's been ages,' Marinas smile faded as he continued, 'thing is, and I hate to be telling you this over the phone, but I'd never forgive myself if I didn't warn you....'

'What is it Clive, you know you can tell me anything.'

'Ok, when I knocked on your door earlier, Roland answered it.'

'Well, he is Ruby's boss, what's wrong, are you worried a

house call means she's getting fired?'

'If only that were the case, I'm sorry Marina, he was in his underwear and I could see Ruby scurrying around trying to get her clothes on'.

Marina let out a short, sad laugh as the light dawned.

NEVER THOUGHT I'D CURSE THE DAY

TJ Spencer & Dean Wrigley

'I tell you, Jim. I never thought I'd curse the day my daughter was born.'

'How do you mean?'

'Well, the wife had gone into labour. I'm on my last delivery of the day in Rothsey Avenue, when this crazy bitch opens the door and claims I'm the father of her kid. She reckons I shagged her five years ago and her daughter's mine. I dunno what to do. The shock would kill the wife if she finds out. I can't even remember meeting this Tania cow.'

'Tania? She had a baby?'

'Yes, a daughter called Lia.'

'Jeez. What are you going to do?'

'I'm going to call her. That's what I'm going to do. It's ringing.'

'Hello Craig? Have you decided she's yours?'

'Look Tania, I don't even know you. How can you be so sure she's mine?'

'Oh, she's yours. We met in *The Wagon*.'

'*The Wagon*? I'm in there now.'

'Are you? I'm outside. I'm coming in.'

The front door of the pub swung open. It's Tania.

Craig watches as Tania looks round the pub. She waves at the two men. Neither one waves back.

'Hiya Craig.'

Tania pauses

'So you going to support me and your kid?'

'I, I, I...'

Craig stutters, and Jim swigs his beer.

'Well, she's yours so...'

'So, hm…'

'Come on, move over.'

Tania squeezes in a seat next to Craig.

'Do you want a drink?'

Jim downs the last drops of beer in his glass, stands and moves toward the bar.

'Well, you know what I like, don't ya!'

Jim goes to the bar, ignoring Tania.

'Pint for you Craigy?'

'Yeah, I need one.'

'Here, why's he calling you Craig?'

Tania looks puzzled.

'Cos that's my name. But you know that already.'

'Nah, nah you're not Craig.'

'Yes, yes, my name is Craig, you know it is Tania.'

'No, that's Craig...'

The woman points at Jim.

'No, that's Jim. I'm Craig.'

'Jim, but he, I, we...' Tania twitches.

'Eh, you what?'

'He said his name was Craig.'

'Nah, that's Jim. My best mate.'

'But I picked up his wallet. Craig's wallet.'

'What? When?'

'Five years ago.'

'Five... what?'

'The night I fell pregnant.'

Tania stands up, slamming her hand on the table. 'Oi you Craig!'

Jim turns round with two pints in his hand.

He's just about to walk back to the table when he looks Tania straight in the eyes.

Then Jim drops the beer glasses.

SMASH! Beer covers the floor and Jim's chinos. He looks like he's wet himself.

'Now you remember me, don't you, you slime ball?'

Tania goes toward Jim.

'You said your name was Craig. I gave you your wallet back, you were pissed out of your head.'

'Nah, nah he's not Craig.'

Craig looks lost. 'Hang on, when was this?' Tania turns toward Craig 'Nearly 6 years ago, 9 months before my Lia was born.'

'But you said I was the father...'

'What no mate, I'd remember you.'

'But you said I was your kid's dad. You even trapped me into delivering a parcel to yours just so you could tell me about my daughter.'

Tania bites her lip then produces a card from her handbag.

'Craig gave me this, after we'd done the biz that night.'
Craig takes the card, flips it over. It's one of his old business
cards from when he was a window cleaner.

'I haven't done window cleaning in at least seven years and I
didn't use these cards five years ago, cos they cost too much to
get printed.'

'Not you, him. It was him, he said his name was Craig. He
gave me that card.'

Tania points to where Jim had stood. Jim had disappeared
from the pub. All that remained was a puddle of beer on the pub
floor.

'Look, that bloke got me up the duff. After I returned his
wallet, he, Craig, bought me a few drinks, we got tiddley. It was
dark that night. He said he'd take me home. We only made it to
the park. That's where we did the biz.'

'What, but how come he had my card?'

'The card was in his wallet. He gave me the card. Said it was
his card.'

Craig goes bright red.

'Jim, Jim, you get your shagging arse back here right now!'

'No, he's called Craig.'

'Craig, come back, Craig, my Lia needs her daddy.
CRAIIIIGGGG!'

NEVER THOUGHT I'D CURSE THE DAY

Daizi Rae

Chris and Dawn spent weeks going through their dad's house, sorting all his stuff into piles. What to keep, what to sell, what to donate, and what they could throw out. While Chris scrutinised everything, looking for clues about who their dad really was, Dawn looked like she really couldn't care less. Not even a little curious about the man that made them.

They waded through their dad's world of fads and short-lived hobbies. In the shed, they found unused gardening tools, art supplies still in the packaging, and a treadmill that still had the price tag attached.

They went through every room in the house with a fine-tooth comb. Treasures appearing in the most unlikely places, like the drum kit buried under a mountain of dirty washing in the back bedroom, along with a guitar case with no guitar and a dusty box full of knitting needles and not so much as one ball of wool in sight.

'Loads of junk to throw out, but loads of stuff to sell too' Chris exclaimed.

'It all looks like he bought it on the cheap to me,' Dawn sighed, and he briefly wondered how she knew.

Chris didn't remember his dad being a bad man. He did some of the stuff that dads do, like teaching Chris to play football, taking them to Goose Fair. He even bought them a rabbit once, not that they ever looked after it, despite the promises. It was just that these things were rare. What he was consistent with was being absent. Starting when they were still little, with missed birthdays, not turning up for school plays at Christmas. By the time Chris was eight, their dad only turned up for a visit once or twice a year. Dawn would slink out without a word, to her mates house and mum would vanish to the kitchen to make tea, leaving Chris to eagerly tell his dad all about what was going well, hoping for a word of praise, which usually came in the form of 'hmm mm,' while he kept an eye on the door.

Dawn left home when Chris was fourteen, and their dad came around even less often after that. Chris did a passable job at faking indifference to his dad's absence as a teenager, and their dad just drifted further and further away. When Dawn got married, they invited their dad to the wedding, but it was Chris she asked to walk her down the aisle.

At Dawn's request, Chris was the one to sort out their dad's bedroom. The bed stank and the furniture in there was mostly empty, just neglected, dusty stuff to throw into bin bags for black bin day. All the clothes that must have been in there once upon a time were now part of the laundry mountain that had been burying the drum kit. Despite his years of faking indifference to his dad's absence, Chris now had carte blanche to dig through every single bit of his dad's life. What that did just added to his lifetime of disappointment. No hidden boxes of treasure to show he'd loved or cherished his children. No photographs, no diary full of what ifs. It all made Chris feel a bit daft.

Last year, it was Dawn that had told Chris dad was ill. 'Oh, by the way,' she added at the very end of their monthly phone call, 'Dad's been in the hospital.' He's ok now, back at home. Listen, don't worry about it…' she trailed off. There was nothing else to say, really.

Chris didn't call back about it, and neither did she. The next time they spoke, she told him, totally devoid of emotion. 'He's dead.'

So here they are, sorting all his stuff into piles. What to keep, what to sell, what to donate and what they could throw out. And in all that stuff, there is nothing to shed any light on who their dad was or why he kept his distance.

Chris lugs bags and boxes out the door with his sister, and wonders why there was no one left who knew him. When they are finished, they stand side by side on the lawn, looking back at the house devoid of life. Chris mutters, 'I should have gone to see him, you know, before…'

Dawn looks at him and slowly shakes her head. She rests her hand on his shoulder, not quite disguising the incredulous look on her face, and for a moment Chris is sure she's about to tell him something he should already know, but all she says it 'see you at Easter little bother.'

And then she's gone without looking back, bounding down the pavement towards her car with a lightness in her step he's never seen before.

A light bulb switched on in Chris's mind along with the tears in his eyes.

NEVER THOUGHT I'D CURSE THE DAY

April Berry

Have you ever looked back in time and pinpointed a day in your life that changed everything - be it in a good way or a bad way? My pivotal moment was a day that started like all others, early morning alarm, shower, breakfast, coffee, commute, everything as normal. Until, one thing changed all that, I caught an earlier bus!

My next-door neighbour was on the bus, but not with her husband. She was snuggled into the back seat of the bus with the wife of another of my neighbours. Taken aback, I didn't know where to look. Were they embarrassed? No, they both said hello to me! At least they kept up the social niceties.

Ten minutes into my journey, a colleague from work joined me on the bus... Oh no... She just talks incessantly, well no more reading for me. As we approached town, I got off earlier than normal. What is happening today? I thought to myself.

As I was walking to work, I passed a coffee shop; the aroma was so enticing that I couldn't resist doubling back and joining the endless queue and treating myself to a nice coffee. I've not been out much lately. Suddenly I heard a commotion behind me and someone ran into the shop waving what at first looked like a baton! My eyes widen when I realised it was in fact a gun. The screams from the queue rang round the shop and reverberated up the street where most of the queue still was.

Suddenly, a loud pop was heard from inside the shop and the guy with the gun came running out. It rooted most of us to the spot, unable to move. You could see differing expressions in people's eyes, shock, fear, a few people were visibly crying. The queue dispersed, leaving only a few of us still there. Adrenaline was coursing through my body. I felt no fear and made my way into the shop, where I noticed a few people crowded behind the counter.

I dialled 999, asked for the police and gave all the details I could. As I had a proper look at the person on the ground, to my horror I recognised her as my next-door neighbour, badly hurt. Her companion was kneeling down beside her.

The ambulance arrived, I gave my statement to the police, and I left the scene to go to work. Some form of normality descended on my day, and I was relieved when I was on my way back home.

Arriving home, I was stopped by my next-door neighbour's husband, who regaled to me everything that had happened to his wife that day, he had just returned apparently from the hospital, where because of covid restrictions he wasn't able to see his wife. I stood and looked at him with a heavy heart. Do I tell him what really happened?

As I left him at the end of his drive, I cursed the day I caught an earlier bus, now I have to live with a secret that isn't mine or risk destroying lives, ruining friendships... do I tell him his wife is having an affair or do I keep quiet and compromise my integrity?

WHY ARE YOU BLUSHING?

Dean Wrigley

We stepped out of the pub, and she led me to a dark backstreet. Belle stopped walking, sat down on a doorstep, and rummaged in her coat pocket. She found her goody tin, opened it and took out the spliff she had rolled earlier in the afternoon. Putting it to her lips, she flicked her zippo and put the flame to the paper, drawing in deeply. She gently exhaled, and a coil of white smoke slowly mixed with the midnight air. She took another drag and handed the joint to me. I took a drag. The taste stung a little, and I coughed gently before taking another drag. That one was smoother. I handed the joint back to her. 'Mmm, just what I needed,' she said. 'Fiona's coming too. She messaged me. She won't be long now.'

A minute later Fiona turned into the street, accompanied by a man. 'Here they are,' said Belle, rising from the step. She kissed her sister on the cheek and introduced me to Neville. We exchanged greetings. Fiona kissed me on the lips and turned to chase after Belle, who had already taken off.

'Do you know about this place Belle's taking us to, Neville?' I said. 'Yeah, it's a place with a bunch of interesting people. Just the right introduction for an out of towner like yourself,' he replied.

Our journey took us along dark, empty streets - far away from the hubbub of the city centre. Eventually, we turned a corner, and I saw a tall building ahead of us with a large, flashing neon sign displaying 'The Pink Shrimp.' The doorman allowed us to pass, and I followed Fiona ascending the stairs, which opened into a large, darkened room. A bar was on the right. Several longhaired women were sitting on bar stools, their stockinged legs reaching the floor thanks to the huge stilettos. Some ugly, well-oiled men were exchanging banter, making the women laugh raucously. As we passed by, Belle signalled to the bartender and shouted, 'Can we get eight beers here, please' pointing to a four-seater table next to a small dance floor. I sat down opposite Fiona. Belle to my left, Neville to my right.

Soft Cell was being piped through the sound system. There

were three women swaying to *Tainted Love* on the dance floor, surrounded by the coloured lights being reflected onto the floor from the mirror ball above their heads. The beers arrived and were placed in the centre of the table. Each of us pulled two towards us and took a swig. I turned and looked again at the women at the bar. Along with the women on the dance floor, I found the view quite pleasing.

'There are some sexy women in here,' I said, as Belle was taking a swig from her beer bottle. As she moved the bottle away from her lips, a grin appeared on her face. 'They're all blokes' she smirked. Shocked, I looked again, but for a little longer this time. I still maintain they were sexy looking women! This revelation made me take more notice of the other people in the room. My eyes settled on a couple of lads over in the corner. They seemed oblivious to anything but each other. Huge smiles on their faces. Heads close together. The action wasn't long in coming and when it did, their kisses were intensely passionate. I stared at them, fascinated. Having only ever been in straight clubs before, I'd never seen two men so into each other. What a sheltered life I had led.

Someone suddenly appeared next to me. I looked up and saw what looked like a drag queen. Her eyes followed mine to the lads in the corner who were still at it. 'Oh, I say, would you look at that? Are you jealous, sweetheart? If you ask nicely, they might let you join in.' I could feel my cheek flushing. 'Blushing? Why are you blushing, sweetheart? Some guys get all the luck. Just goes to show: when you walk into the pink shrimp you might walk out with a king prawn, if you're lucky.'

'Hello Belle, long time no see. Where have you been hiding, sweetheart?'

'Hi Roxy,' said Belle. 'I've been away. Met this one,' pointing at me, 'thought I'd bring him for a show. It's on tonight, isn't it?'

'Yes. It's a bit late starting. It won't be long.'

Ten minutes later and the show was in full swing. Three nuns had appeared on stage. The spotlights found them and they threw themselves into a rendition of *Rescue Me*. Two backing singers who swayed in time to the music flanked the lead singer.

Songs from *Sister Act* and *The Sound of Music* followed, and the show ended with *Climb Every Mountain*. As the final song ended, the nuns disappeared backstage. The cheers and applause rang around the room, and eventually they were enticed back for an encore. They had all dropped their habits and replaced them with spangly leotards topped off with pink crowns of huge feather plumes.

The show ended, and slowly the people left. We four gathered outside. 'So how was that for you?' asked Neville.

'It was an education, that's for sure,' I said, giggling inside to myself. Fancy them trying to shock me. Me! Life is for living and it takes all sorts to make a world. Embrace the difference. Find the humour, and your life can be so much fun.

WHY ARE YOU BLUSHING?

Carolyn Ward-Daniels

My neighbour Sylvia has popped round for a cuppa and a chat. Thank heavens because Bill can only talk football and gardening. 'Where's that husband of yours, Barbara?' she says 'is he down the pub?'

Before I can speak, Bill comes through the door. 'Thought I heard your voice, Sylvia.'

'Thought you were down the pub.'

'Might as well, get me away from her nagging.'

'I don't nag, do you want a cuppa?'

'No ta, I'm tidying me shed.'

I saw him wink at Silvia and guessed he really was going to the pub. He was either working on nights, in his shed or in the pub. We chatted about all things soaps, but Sylvia really talked about what the characters were wearing rather than the storyline. She was obsessed with clothes, at sixty-one, she was very stylish. Kept her hair tinted a blonde, whereas mine was riddled with grey. Makes me feel a bit scruffy sometimes. I went to let her out, and she turned and said, 'oh did you enjoy the Banana cake?' I said nothing because I couldn't remember any cake and must have looked vacant. 'The cake I made for you?'

I didn't want to look stupid, so I said 'Oh sorry yes thank you.'

She left, hooking her bag over her shoulder. I closed the door and went to the pantry to search for evidence of cake because for the life of me, I couldn't remember it. I went to the loo and the cold tap was running; it had happened before, that worried me too. I asked Bill about the cake and he said he enjoyed it. I had to lie down. Am I going insane? Is dementia knocking on my door? There are other things like finding framed photographs turned round and ornaments changing places. If I don't calm myself, I'll get a bad head. I have to take myself to a happy place. I go back to childhood and I think how would I crayon Bill. Light blue for his faded jeans, a black T-shirt with a scar of red and yellow rock band logo, with his shoulder length hair, he looks like an ancient 70s roadie. Sylvia would have yellow hair and black-rimmed eyes and a floral frock. I couldn't draw me. They didn't make beige crayons.

Today I am going shopping and I am making a list and I am going to tick them off when I put them in the trolley because things I am sure I have bought previously have disappeared from the pantry. I put the receipt in my purse instead of throwing it away. I shelved the shopping, and it felt like I was in a video on repeat. I had done it so many times before.

I found Sylvia's shoulder bag in the lounge; I knew this really worried Bill because I could read it on his face. He said as much as well. 'But... but Barb, can't you remember Sylvia coming round? I dunno lass, you keep leaving taps running, cursing that ornaments are moving themselves. I'll take her bag over. I really think you ought to see somebody.'

Bill was shaking his pink face as he picked up the bag. And I could have cried. 'For Christ's sake, don't tell her I can't remember her visit!'

'I won't.' The tears came. I had no recollection of Sylvia's visit; I thought I'd been out shopping. The other day, the next-door neighbour mentioned Sylvia calling and I couldn't remember that visit either. This is really frightening, I cannot recall. I went to the kitchen and even before I got to the door, I could hear it, the tap. I'd done it again. I would make an appointment to see the doctor. I was sure I had been shopping.

Checking the pantry, there was no rice pudding or baked beans. No tinned tomatoes and I am sure I bought two. The receipt, I found my purse, there was what I knew I'd bought and, of course, the date and the time. Woah! What is going on? It felt like cutlery screeching across a plate. I shuddered.

I looked over at Sylvia's house. Bill should be on his way back, but no sign. I found his beloved shed keys. Inside his large playroom was spotless and mingled with a wood aroma, was a slight perfume. There were a couple of what looked like yoga mats tucked under a bench, made me smile. He'd never done yoga in his life. An assortment of tired furniture had found its end of life here, still functioning as storage. I opened the pale oak wardrobe; it was like a larder, shelves of food. Tesco wouldn't have missed it, but I certainly had. Well, well, if mental cruelty were currency, I'd be married to a rich man, but not for much longer! All the angst and worry over the last few months turned to rage. I ran back to the house to have words, but still he wasn't back.

I wrote a note 'GONE SHOPPING,' then I scooped up the shopping bags and my coat. Quickly, I put the car in the garage, leaving my coat in the car. I went and hid in the downstairs loo off the hall. Just as I stopped panting, I heard him come in and then the blip blip of him texting. As he shuffled off his shoes, his phone rang. 'She's gone shopping again,' he laughed, 'we could have had a bit longer. I'll go and move a few ornaments around she'll be ready to commit herself before Christmas, so where do you fancy it mine or yours Sylvia?'

I chose this moment to come out of hiding. His face is a picture and rouge. 'Sylvia, I have to go.'

'Oh yes, you do, Bill, and now! Why are you blushing?'

WHY ARE YOU BLUSHING?

April Berry

Sarah sat on the settee, at yet another family gathering she would prefer not to be at. She was listening to her cousin Wendy and her husband Giles discussing the latest gossip amongst their friends. It wasn't really Sarah's thing to gossip, but all her family seemed to think it was ok. Although Wendy portrayed herself as very self-righteous.

It was always the same at every family gathering: bitch, bitch, bitch. Sarah wandered off into her own world, and also Giles's and Wendy's. They were all very different people; she sometimes couldn't really believe that she and Wendy were related. Wendy thought herself so superior to the rest of the family, perhaps because her parents were quite wealthy, and Sarah's family just made ends meet and enjoyed what they could afford. Though Sarah was always dubious about the family wealth, not sure it actually came their way from entirely honest means.

Sarah was brought back to reality by Wendy asking what she thought about the lodge that she and Giles were booking for their wedding anniversary. Sarah made all the right noises. She didn't really care where they were going, though she had to admit it looked amazing, just the sort of place that she and Judith would enjoy, if they could afford it. Wendy explained they were going with the children and their good friends, Laurence and Natalie. Judith, Sarah's partner, called them the 4 stooges.

Sarah hated Natalie. They were in the same year at school, and Natalie had made Sarah's life hell. Natalie knew Sarah was Wendy's cousin and rubbed it in her face that she couldn't afford to go on the school skiing trips, as Sarah's parents just couldn't afford it. And Natalie hadn't changed, just more subtle with the barbed comments now.

The next morning, Sarah woke up, full of excitement. She and Judith were going into town to watch a show, have a meal, and then meet up with a few of their friends for a quiet drink.

They both thought the show was amazing, fantastic food and the company of their friends was just the tonic Sarah needed after last night.

Suddenly Sarah looked up. She felt really uneasy and soon knew why. Into the pub walked Wendy alone. She was puzzled. Why was Wendy so far from home and without Giles? Sarah watched Wendy order a drink and find a table. Sarah was certain that Wendy hadn't spotted her, which was just as well because the person who joined Wendy was Laurence!

Sarah was gob smacked, more so when she saw how they were behaving. It was totally apparent that Wendy was having an affair with her best friends husband. She said nothing to Judith, as Judith knew how upset Sarah could get when she was in the company of the 4 stooges.

A couple of weeks passed, and it was Wendy's fathers' birthday, another one of those family get-togethers. After the night at the pub, Sarah didn't want to go. She knew she wouldn't be able to look Wendy in the eye and it would be even worse, as she knew Laurence and Natalie would also be there. Sarah had struggled with the knowledge of her cousin having an affair and could not look them in the eye without turning bright red.

On arrival, Sarah and Judith greeted her uncle, giving him his gift and card. They went to grab a drink in the kitchen and as they entered; they heard Wendy and Natalie discussing Sarah and Judith's relationship in front of all the family, and it wasn't pleasant. Sarah stopped at the kitchen door. She was mortified. Turning to Judith, she could feel herself getting redder and redder in the face. Why did she have to turn this shade of puce when she was angry?

Natalie turned and saw Sarah in the doorway and said, 'well it's about time you knew what the family thinks about your relationship. We all think that you don't deserve Judith.'

Sarah was beside herself. This was the last straw. People in glass houses shouldn't throw bricks… She imparted to the room, which was full of family and friends, including Laurence and Giles. Her knowledge of Wendy and Lawrence's affair turned and walked out of the kitchen with a parting shot…. 'Wendy, why are you blushing?'

WHY ARE YOU BLUSHING?

Daizi Rae

As Walter pulled away from Millie, she sighed and bit down on her bottom lip. She was overcome with emotion. Maybe even the first flush of falling in love. 'Was that even possible this soon?' His love making was so slow and sensual, like he wanted it to last forever, and she was the only woman in the world. Meeting Walter had been the best thing to happen to her since her husband Norman had taken manipulative control of their marriage, on their wedding night, ten years ago. He was out of her life now though, god rest his soul.

Walter gazed back at her flushed, smiling face and congratulated himself on his latest conquest. Millie was quite the looker, and single mums, desperate for a bit of adult attention were always his best bet. His sob story had been tried and tested so many times now, he almost believed it himself. It worked like a charm. He told each one a slightly unique version of it, but the essentials were always the same. His wife had died, and sometimes he just couldn't quite bring himself to stay in the family house surrounded by their life together, so he bought himself a tourer with no heartbreaking memories attached. Walter on Wheels he'd joke, while contriving to look a little heartbroken at the same time. He sure had perfected that vulnerable look. At forty-five, he was getting more sex than he ever did in his twenties. He didn't feel even a twinge of guilt at how betrayed or hurt his wife Ann would feel. If only she knew how many times he had killed her off, just to get his end away. This latest one was even a friend of Ann's sister Jenny. Risky, but he couldn't resist a red head.

Walter gently swept a stray lock of Millie's auburn hair off her face and leaned in to kiss her lips, the tip of her nose and her forehead as he gently put pressure on her shoulders to ease her into position to pleasure him. He buried his face in her hair as she complied, so she wouldn't see the smug look on his face. Walter was living his best life right now.

The tourer shifted slightly as Ann stepped in and coughed to get their attention. Millie giggled in embarrassment at being caught out by a stranger. She was flustered and trying to straighten her clothes. In her distraction it didn't occur to her to wonder why this woman had let herself into Walters' tourer. She looked at Walter, watching as colour flooded his face. She was about to tease him for blushing when Ann snapped with disdain, 'Another one Walter, Really! And you, whatever your name is, actually, don't tell me. I really don't need to know. What line did he use this time? He's been widowed for a couple of years, but getting to know you has made him realise life isn't over?'

Millie stood speechless, blushing to her roots as the penny dropped. Frustration and humiliation taking over from where the possibilities of falling in love had so recently been. She just wanted the floor to open up and swallow her whole. Much like she'd been about to do for whatever Walter gave her. She grabbed her coat and her bag, intent on getting out of there as fast as possible. Before she left, she quietly slid a knitting needle out of her bag and into Walter's stomach.

Ann smiled to herself as the tourer door shut behind the departing Millie. She owed Jenny a drink for this one.

DON'T BE EMBARRASSED, IT'S NORMAL

Daizi Rae

Pretending she was a Jedi this morning walking through that automatic sliding door, chatting about her day with you, her favourite dog in the entire world, who looks just like an Ewok, was enough to make my heart skip a beat. It was the most normal thing in the world to you two. However, if you had looked around at the other humans using that same door, you'd have seen a mixture of judgy ones nudging one another as they sniggered. And kindred spirits, who definitely do the same thing and just get it. There may even have been one or two that just quietly sighed, shaking their heads at you.

Not me, I totally get it. They may choose to believe that little Ruby doesn't understand language, she's just a dog, and that blank look they see is her just waiting for her next treat or her favourite tummy tickle, but what do they know, right! What is your human supposed to do? Just ignore you when you ask her a question?

I've been watching you both for days now. I've seen the conversations you two have, and I really want to be a part of your world. So I'm going to 'accidentally' bump into you again in the park later. I just need to stick to my plan. I'm gonna walk past you when you walk in the gate, close enough for you not to miss me. Like I do every day lately. When you stop to sniff your favourite bench and your human has a sit down, I'm gonna be casually laying down nearby, showing you my tummy, so you know I'm all yours, and I think you're so cute, all fur and sass. You growled at me the first couple of days, but yesterday I swear you looked for me before you got there. I'm gonna try a playful nip at you today and see if you like to play chase. I love to play chase. I'll chase balls or sticks or ducks off the pond. I'm fantastic at it. I want to show you how fast I am today.

I'm here, I'm ready. Are you coming? Are you nearly here? I'm waiting for you. I can see the ducks and I'm leaving them alone, in case you want to chase them with me today. Come on Ruby, and your human. I want her to like me, too.

Oh, I can see you, there you are, all jaunty, your little nose up in the air, your tail bouncing from side to side, so, so cute. Your ears pick up and I think you've seen me. I pant a little faster and try my hardest to wait for you to catch me up. I can't go running up to you yet, that's just not cool is it, so I'm patiently waiting for you to get to your favourite bench, then I'll saunter out from behind this tree to lie down and show you my tummy.

It's time. You're at the bench. You're here, sat looking up at your human, all attentive, hanging off every word she says. She must be very special. I like her too. If you do, then I do. I'm hers too. She just doesn't know it yet. I make my way to your side and roll over as always. Oh joy of joys, you come over and lay your head on my tummy, my heart wants to explode. When you sit up again, I sit too and bark once at you, nip at you, and bounce back a couple of steps to see if you want to come and play chase with me. Today is the best day ever, because here you come and we both chase round and round the bench, switching directions until I'm not sure who is chasing who any more. It's wonderful. Your human is laughing, shouting encouragement to let us play longer, 'go get him Ruby' and 'go on little fella.' She likes me, she really likes me.

***

Annabeth walked her dog Ruby through the park most days, and had made a point of stopping at this one bench every day, for the last week or so. She'd noticed a skittish, skinny little black dog that seemed to make a beeline for them, hovering just out of reach. Annabeth was a patient woman. She loved animals, and this little fella had caught her attention as he crawled out from under the bushes in the park every day, like he lived there. He never seemed to be with anyone, and Annabeth worried about him. He looked like he needed a good meal, and she couldn't see any sign of a collar.

Today Annabeth had a spare harness and lead with her. She hoped that the little fella was still here. Yesterday he'd come quite close and laid down submissively, showing his tummy to Ruby, but he still seemed a little wary, and Annabeth didn't want to scare him away before he was ready. The little fella really seemed quite taken with Ruby and today he went from submissive to playful, as the two dogs played chase round and round the bench she was sitting on. It was a joy to watch.

Annabeth put down a bowl of water for the two panting dogs, and while they had their fill, she quietly slipped the spare harness on the little fella and gently attached the lead.

***

'Oh my gosh, oh my gosh, they like me, they really like me. Look at me in a harness and on a lead. I have a family; it worked!'

DON'T BE EMBARRASSED, IT'S NORMAL

April Berry

Why do I always blush at the slightest thing? If it's anything out of the ordinary, regardless of what it is, I end up with a bright red face, feeling embarrassed, shy and shuffling from foot to foot, wishing the ground would open and swallow me. This has been going on for years, resulting in me missing so much that life offers. I became embarrassed by my embarrassment.

Chatting with Julie about my predicament over a beer one spring afternoon, she suggested hypnotherapy. 'What,' I exclaimed, 'how will that help? I would be so embarrassed if anyone found out.'

'No, you wouldn't,' Julie retorted 'I've done my research and hypnotherapy can help with many things. Including blushing at everything, you are the only person I know who blushes at people holding hands.'

After internet researching for most of the evening, I had contact details of a couple of hypnotists, both with glowing references. Oh well, here goes I thought the next morning, stood in the middle of the kitchen with mobile in hand. Eventually, after calls with both hypnotists, who both sounded like they had never been embarrassed in their life, I made an appointment. The longest two days of my life, spent yo-yoing between, I can do this and I can't do this. The visit went well, as did the subsequent five, though to be honest I didn't feel any different apart from my bank balance... blimey, they aren't cheap...

On reflection, looking back, I had a fantastic summer. Julie and I went to Italy on holiday, and I never noticed that I wasn't blushing. I danced with strange guys in Milan, talked to a geeky guy on the train ride from Milan to Rome, chatted with a lovely married couple on the flight home. I went with a group of friends to a few music festivals, I plucked up the courage to talk to strangers at the pub and in the cinema queue. All things that twelve months ago, would have turned me bright red and into a complete nervous wreck.

When I visited my parents, they both commented on how much more confidence I had these days. And that they always knew I would grow out of my habit of blushing. I didn't have the heart, nor the courage, to admit that I had been to a hypnotist, knowing that my parents didn't really believe in that kind of thing.

Returning to school after the summer holidays, I need to add I'm a teacher, not a student. I couldn't believe the fantastic summer I had just had and was admitting as much to Julie one evening after the first week of school. I also felt a lot more confident at school. Oh, I knew previously that it didn't take students long to realise I blushed at the slightest little thing and they took full advantage of it.

Julie had a strange look on her face, what's up I enquired. She took a deep breath and quietly said, 'what's up? Don't you remember half of what you did this summer?'

'What do you mean,' I asked, I was concerned that something was matter with Julie as she continued in a quiet voice.

'Do you really think that your behaviour this summer has been normal? You accosted a guy in a nightclub in Milan and kissed him right in front of his girlfriend. You put your bra and shorts in a guy's rucksack on the train to Rome and wondered why he complained. You slept in some poor guy's sleeping bag at one festival and complained when he wouldn't join you. You gate crashed a porn studio in Rome and asked to be in the film. Not to mention all the other embarrassing things you have done in the last seven weeks, and whenever I said anything to you, all you could say to me was, don't be embarrassed, it's normal! Absolutely nothing you have done this summer has been normal. Where's the telephone number of that hypnotist you went to?'

UNDER THE BED

Gerry O'Keeffe

My heart was beating out a samba against my rib cage. It felt like it was crushing the oxygen supplies to my brain. I couldn't breathe! Sweat was bursting from every pore. It was my birthday, and I was under my bed looking for my presents, when I saw it, glowing with strange writing that danced across the wrapping paper to the rhythm of my heartbeat.

Then I heard it whisper. 'Open my pages to discover my wonder and magic within.' Still shaking, I crawled slowly towards the present and gazed upon its strange wrapping paper. The writing seemed to stop moving and form words in English. Which read, open me to discover my magic within.

Once I gathered my breath, I tentatively, but with a lot of curiosity, opened the package. Inside was this amazing alien looking leather-bound book. However, instead of normal pages, I discovered each page within was a mirror. Each mirrored page reflected various adventures at different stages of my lifetime.

The first image I glanced upon was a webbed creature with gills on its neck, standing in a blue lagoon, holding a trident. In the next, I was a teenager sporting a boarding school uniform, wearing glasses with long flowing hair covering my strange, shaped ears. Then I turned into a superhero with a cape and an alien crest on my chest that shape shifted periodically. The next page portrayed me in my late twenties, dressed like Dr. Jackal, then turning into Mr. Hyde.

It was heartening to discover that there were also normal reflections too. Me as a footballer holding a trophy aloft. Another at my wedding with an unrecognisable beautiful brunette beside me. The pages showed children in my life, growing up before my eyes. In fact, my entire life seems to live out in front of me on those pages.

Flicking back to the first mirrored page, I discovered other adventures. Hunting with that trident, meeting a beautiful girl, falling in love and saving her life. Each page I turned, adventure after adventure, played out before me, one after another, mesmerising me, until it lost me in time. That is until I got to the last mirror. It shocked me to see myself as an old man still under the bed. I slowly moved my hand to my face, and the reflection did the same. To my horror, I could feel the wrinkles on my face.

I snapped the book closed and slowly crawled back out from under the bed. I was covered in cobwebs! I screamed! My brothers' skeleton was on the bed beside mine, spiders crawling all over his cobwebbed corpse. I looked out of the window. My reflection stared back at me, which was still old and wrinkled. Looking past the reflection, it appeared the apocalypse had happened while I was under that bed. Everywhere was in ruins. Spaceships crashed on the ground, rotting alien and human corpses scattered everywhere. And throughout this I had been safe under the bed, living life after life of adventure and wonder.

While gathering my thoughts on the scene in front of me, the room spun, and the floor fell beneath me. It seemed I was falling through space. Everything went black. After what felt like forever, I heard a voice and found I was being shaken and woken up.

It was my brother. 'Happy Birthday Bro.' He handed me this present, 'have a look at what I've bought you.' I slowly looked around me. Relief washed over me as I looked around at normal surroundings. Looking at my brother, anticipation and excitement washing over me, I gasped as my brother handed me the present from my dreams.

UNDER THE BED

Carolyn Ward-Daniels

Bradley was making fun of his sister and mum, the latter watching the film through her platted fingers and his sister peeping over a cushion as if it would make it less scary. Even with his taunts of 'it's not real,' he wished he wasn't watching 'Pet Cemetery'. The under the bed scene made him physically jump. He couldn't lose face now, so he had to watch. At 22, he was the only man in the house and his mum and younger sister ran around after him, which actually made him the weakest. He never cooked, laundered, cleaned, or helped in any way. He didn't know how much a loaf of bread or a pint of milk cost. Any girls he dated gave up on him after realising he couldn't pick up after himself and didn't even try.

Bradley was relieved when the film finished, and he retired to bed. As soon as he walked into his bedroom, the dark gap under the bed scared him. He leapt into bed from two feet away, not daring to get his ankles close. He thought about the terrified faces of the victims being chased, but how must the perpetrator have felt, not scared, excited even. He then thought how would he feel being in a wood alone at night and would he be scared if he was the perpetrator. These musings excited him and he imagined following a lone girl under the cover of darkness, of her becoming aware and petrified and running and him driving the fear. He found this unbelievably exciting. Where would this place be? What would he wear? He hated walking in the dark alone, but this would be different. People would be scared of him. This would give him steel. He thought about the local area; he had grown up there and he knew the parks, walks and short cuts. He went to sleep dreaming about it. He woke up thinking about his proposed adventure. It would make him fearless.

He put a black bandana in his hoody pocket to use as a face mask if the opportunity arose; he hadn't got a clue how it would. Then one evening his 17-year-old sister Penny had a girlfriend turn up. They spent an hour in Penny's room and at just gone nine Bradley heard Penny and her friend clattering downstairs; he was just sauntering to the kitchen. Penny said, 'Bradley, can you walk Vicki part way home? She's running a bit late, and she doesn't like going through the park on her own.'

'Why don't you go?'

'I've homework, she lied.'

Bradley begrudgingly asked where she lived. 'On the Manford estate on the other side of the park, I said I'd be home for 9 so I haven't got time to go around the park, but I don't like the wooded bit it creeps me out.'

Bradley smelled the whiff of fear and said, 'Yeah, alright.'

'Just to the other park gates, then I'll be fine.'

He pulled on his hoody and they set off. Vicki talked about her favourite music, which Bradley wasn't into. He was more interested in her nervous glances at the clumps of bushes lining the path. Three of the five lamps had been broken, so it was dark. She thanked him a little way from the gates and they parted.

Now it was his turn to be nervous. This was his test. He could have gone out of the park and gone the long way round, but he wanted to challenge himself and he dared himself to go into the wooded area.

As soon as he left the path and he was hidden, his nerves calmed because he was the perpetrator. The moon was a sliver on its back so there was little light; He shone his phone torch just to settle himself. Then he heard voices. He pulled out the black bandana and tied it as a face mask and pulled over his hood.

He heard two girls giggling, one saying, 'I know first I didn't expect her, then I didn't think she was going to go.'

'I saw her turn up and waited ages for her to leave. She hates me, thinks I stole her boyfriend, anyway see you tomorrow.'

'See ya.'

Bradley couldn't believe his luck. He had a choice of two victims. His trial run may as well be on the way home, he thought, closer to get away. His pulse gathered speed as he made his move. A twig snapped under his foot and he saw the dark shape of the girl stop a couple of seconds and then she started walking fast and he hurried through the bushes, the noises sounded so loud and the girl picked up pace and so did he his adrenalin bubbling. He heard a little cry some 30 metres ahead, and he nearly stopped but couldn't. His head was buzzing, this is what it feels like, so much control, he sprang onto the path, the girl looked round and then ran crying, 'no, no, no.'

He chased on and then he thought what was he going to do when he caught her and stopped. He then realised she would tell someone and he would be the hunted. He ripped off the bandana and stuffed it deep into a bush. He turned and ran all the way back to where he had parted with Vicki and took the long way home.

When he reached home, a police car was parked outside. He broke out in a sweat. 'They can't know it's me, surely.' He dawdled through the front door and found a policewoman and his mum comforting his sister, who was sobbing and shaking. Penny looked petrified.

UNDER THE BED

April Berry

Phew! That was a close call. I was nearly caught and only just made my escape. But at least I have food now, which should last me for a couple of weeks. It's been a strange year. Everybody has been at home. No one has been going out anywhere, not even to work. For someone who relies on empty houses to ensure that I can eat and sleep, it has been very stressful. Not that my life is peaceful at the best of times. I am viewed as a pariah, along with all the other tragic souls who don't own or rent their home.

Don't get me wrong, it's not all bad. At least, through my stealth, I can sleep indoors even though it can be difficult at times.

My heart pounding, I start to eat my spoils when I see two beady eyes peering at me… Oh no, it's Clive. You might remember Clive from Christmas. I hated him; he knew where I lived and did his utmost to let everyone else in the house know about my presence. Not that anyone took any notice of him. He was a bit of a hooligan, and obviously being a cat, he couldn't talk, so the inhabitants of the house just ignored him. He couldn't get to me, as the space wasn't big enough for him to squeeze through, although he spent hours trying. He was the major reason that I normally only came out for food every few days, when he was out and the coast was clear.

The only person who knew of my existence, apart from Clive, was Shaun, the youngest member of the household. He spent quite a long time talking with me and promised to always protect me. And it was under Shaun's bed that I lived.

Now I am quite an astute little chap. After all, I have brought over a thousand offspring into the world, looking after them as babies and sending them into the big wide world as adults. I overheard a conversation that the husband was having on his mobile. Now my hearing is exceptional. I do have 8 ears after all. Well, technically not ears, they are on my legs, and the conversation was interesting. I worked out that the husband was hiding something from his wife and it was in the ottoman space under Shaun's mattress. I wasn't the only one who overheard the conversation, so did the wife. The ensuing mayhem was quite comical to watch. I crept out from my hiding space to watch the missiles flying around the bedroom. Poor Shaun was pressed up against the wall in his bedroom, tears streaming down his face as he watched his parents throwing all his star wars figures at each other. As they slammed against the wall, they shattered into pieces with the force of each throw.

Shaun started screaming, watching his toys being thrown by his parents, none of them contacting with the intended target. Shaun's sister ran into the room to see what was happening. I crept out a little further to get a better view and the next thing I saw were gleaming white, sharp columns coming towards me and closing over my body. Trapping me in a prison I couldn't escape from, my legs were battling outside the cage bars, trying to get a grip to escape. Peering out from the white barred prison, I saw Shaun coming towards me. 'Clive, drop him,' he screamed. Shaun was trying to save me. He made a lunge for Clive, who turned away from Shaun.

This was the last thing I remembered before the sharp white pillars pierced my body and everything went black.

UNDER THE BED

Daizi Rae

I want to tell you a story that was told to me by my doddery old neighbour Gladys. I'll warn you up front, Gladys was not what you would call reliable, or even honest most of the time. She spun a good yarn though, and whether or not they were true; they were entertaining as hell. I'd soaked them up like a sponge for the whole five years I'd lived next door to her. Even looked forward to them, if I'm honest. This particular story was delivered on bated breath, while her eyes darted round like she was waiting to be reprimanded for daring to repeat such words. She was a true drama queen. I loved it. When I got off the bus on the way home from work and saw Gladys lurking in her front garden, I grinned to myself, thinking, ooh, here we go. I'd barely got the garden gate shut behind me before she launched into it with that gleam in her eye.

'Ooh, I'm glad you're home. I just got off the phone to our Pearl.'

'Oh yeah, how is she?' I asked with a smile. She was a pleasant woman, Pearl. All smiles and ample bosom. She made a mean apple pie.

'Let me tell ya,' she beamed, before lowering her voice like we were co-conspirators in some secret service shenanigans. 'Did I ever tell you about our Pearls' youngest, Sharon? Just divorced from that no good shit she's been married to for far too long. Anyway, she just moved into a new flat up the high street, got one of them communal doors that shuts behind you and locks itself. So, anyway, she went down there to pick up her mail, chatting on the phone to our Pearl, telling her all about the flat.

When she got back, she sat on the bed to open her mail, still on the phone to our Pearl. Well, anyway, she dropped it on the floor. The phone, I mean, and it slid under the bed. She had to lie on the floor to get it, when summat caught her eye. There was only someone under the bed!'

'Oh, my god.' I gasped.

'It terrified her. He was lying dead still, with his back to her, not moving a muscle. Pearl said, how Sharon didn't scream, she'll never know. There must have been so many thoughts rushing through her head. But she stayed proper calm and played it brilliantly.'

'Bloody hell, Gladys, what did she do?'

'She picked up her phone, that's what she did, and said to our Pearl, "Sorry mum, I dropped my phone, I'm just gonna get a quick shower and I'll call you back." The bathroom is right by her bed, so she went in and quietly locked the door behind her. She turned on the shower and climbed out the window and called the police. Damn lucky she didn't move into the third floor, is all I can say, she'd have broken her bloody legs jumping out that window!

I'm shaking just thinking about it. The police told her not to go back in, like she needed telling that, but to wait for them across the street. So she sort of hovered across the road, monitoring the bathroom window and seeing if anyone came out of the front door of the building.

She called our Pearl back while she waited for the police, and you know she was round there in a flash. Got there right before the police did. They were right on the ball, straight in the building to see what was what. They were only in there a couple of minutes, when two of them came out holding a skinny, scruffy looking fella. His eyes looked crazy, but he didn't try to get away, probably didn't have the strength. The officer that had stood with Sharon, while the police searched her flat (she was a right mess by then, shivering and crying) told her they'd found the man stood outside her bathroom door, holding one of her kitchen knives, waiting for her to come out.

He'd crept in the entry door while she was getting her mail and hid under the bed. Turns out he was a homeless person. If they don't lock him up in a mental hospital after this, then I don't know what! The police told our Pearl that what our Sharon did was truly amazing. If she had screamed when she saw him, this could've ended so differently.'

'Wow, she's lucky she's still here to tell the tale, Gladys. Are you going over to...'

Just then we could hear Gladys' phone ringing insistently from in the house.

'I better get that,' she said, all wide eyed. She turned and shuffled her way up the path towards her front door. As she got to the door, she looked over her shoulder and warned me, 'check under your bed tonight dear, good neighbours are hard to come by.'

SLEEPWALKING

Dean Wrigley

Professor Plum sat bolt upright in bed. He reached towards the bedside cabinet, grabbed his spectacles, unfolded them, and placed them on his face. He got out of bed and wandered around the walls, eventually finding the door. In the pitched darkness, he fumbled for the doorknob and turned it. He opened the door and turned right into a corridor.

Walking a few steps, he brushed against a wooden cabinet, stopped and turned towards it. He looked through the cabinet's double glass doors, his eyes darting over the objects on the cabinet shelves.

Opening the glass doors, his right hand took hold of a wooden box and lifted it towards him. There was a little key in the lock. He turned the key, opened the box, and took out a small pistol.

He lifted the pistol, placed it against his temple, and squeezed the trigger. Nothing. He pumped the trigger a few more times, but nothing more than a weak spray of water puffed from the barrel. Empty.

He put the pistol down and descended the staircase. He entered a room containing a large table with the remnants of a banquet strewn across it and a lone candlestick in the centre. Propped up against the candlestick was a Polaroid photograph. He picked it up and looked at it. It had been taken recently. He recognised himself in it. Colonel Mustard, Mrs. Peacock and the flame-haired Miss Scarlett. The other names slipped his mind. He went to place the picture back on the table, but it dropped from his hand and fluttered to the floor.

He picked up a knife from the table. He held it by the handle, pointing it downwards and began stabbing at the oranges in the fruit bowl. As each orange was punctured, some juice squirted out and splashed onto his hand. He dropped the knife, and it landed point first on the photograph, pinning it to the laminate floor and vibrating menacingly upon the image of Miss Scarlett.

Another door. He opened it and went into an untidy store cupboard. His rapid eyes saw a large spanner hanging from a nail in the wall and leaning up against the wall was a long pipe. He picked up the pipe and pulled it towards him. Henry swivelled around with a hollow sliding sound and viewed him suspiciously with an enormous pair of surprised eyes.

A rope was hanging from a hook in the cupboard ceiling. He pulled it off the hook, gauged its length in his hands and tied a knot in its centre. He tugged at it to tighten the knot. He reversed out of the cupboard and walked back to the hallway, dominated by a large mirror. In the mirror, he saw a man wearing purple pyjamas and an urge to do him physical harm arose in the professor's psyche.

He wrapped the rope around the man's neck and pulled on both ends. The rope tightened and the eyes of the man in the mirror bulged, his tongue came out of his mouth and he even got a little sexually aroused. The professor laughed at that, coughed and dropped the rope. He turned and climbed the staircase, rubbing at the discomfort in his throat.

He wandered back along the corridor, hugging the wall, and found a doorknob. He turned the knob, opened the door, and walked into the room. His bare foot kicked against a pillow that had been thrown on the floor. He picked it up, restored its plumpness and removed a long red hair from it before placing it over her sleeping face and pressing down firmly until her struggling had ceased.

He left the bedroom where the corpse of Miss Scarlett was cooling under a pillow and crossed the corridor into his own bedroom. He climbed into bed and settled his head.

Moments later, he felt something digging into him from behind his ears and across the bridge of his nose. He awoke with a start and realised he was wearing his spectacles. His hands were sticky, his throat was sore and his hair was damp on one side.

'Oh no, I've been sleepwalking again, and it feels like I've been up to some mischief,' he said to himself. 'I hope nobody guesses who did it, where they did it and with what.'

SLEEPWALKING

Daizi Rae

Natalie shrugged on her favourite mustard coloured coat as she absentmindedly sized up the wall above the antique Delft Jardinière she had acquired just yesterday. She knew exactly what they needed for that space, and she knew just where to get it. She stepped outside and looked up at a sky full of sparkling stars as she made her way to the Rue de Rivoli to pick up the perfect little painting for her wall.

The door to the gallery was unlocked, so Natalie slipped inside, her footsteps echoing back at her as she made her way through the empty hallways towards her prize. Oh, and there she was, all 77x53cm of her, the ideal dimensions, and the love of her life was her namesake. It was fate, surely.

She'd read somewhere that if you behaved as if you belonged, you were a lot less likely to have your actions questioned, so she confidently lifted her painting of choice off the wall, she didn't bother to wrap it in anything, or try to hide it. Natalie left the Louvre, closed the door behind her and turned left off the Rue de Rivoli onto Mayfield Grove. She entered her house and hung her new painting in pride of place above the Jardinière.

She made herself a cup of tea and stood in the lounge doorway, blowing the steam from her drink and admiring her acquisition with a contented smile. Her home was now complete. She washed up her favourite Tiffany teacup, made her way to bed and drifted into the satisfied sleep of the accomplished.

As Natalie woke up, she yawned, stretched and opened her eyes, immediately squinting at the sunshine streaming through the bare window in their huge empty bedroom full of promise. A grin slowly crept across her face as she sat up and slid her arms around her new wife. On this, their first morning waking up together in their new home. I think we should paint this room cornflower blue to match your beautiful eyes, she whispered, as she kissed her wife's bare shoulder. Lisa turned to kiss Natalie and smiled as she slipped out of bed

'Lots of white and maybe a little dusky pink would look

amazing with that blue for this room baby, good call'. She dropped her wife a saucy wink as she sashayed naked across the bedroom, picking up her dressing gown from the floor, where she had abandoned it in her rush to christen their marital bed the night before.

'I'm going to unpack the cups and see if I can find the teapot. We deserve a decent brew before we get started with decorating and unpacking.' Natalie groaned playfully at the thought of all the work to be done and snuggled back under the duvet to wait for her morning tea to arrive.

As Lisa padded through to the kitchen on her hunt for the teapot, she noticed the front door was ajar. Her stomach dropped in fear. Had someone been in the house? Oh god! What if they were still here? She stopped dead in her tracks and held her breath, trying to listen for any sounds of movement in the rest of the house. She couldn't hear anything, so she crept through to the kitchen. There was no one there. As she turned to creep into the lounge to check there, she realised how stupid it was for her to go looking for an intruder. What did she think she'd do if she found one? But she carried on regardless. Luckily for her, there was no one else in the house. What she found instead was a painting hanging on the lounge wall that hadn't been there when they'd gone to bed last night. With a puzzled look on her face and her mind whirling through possible scenarios, both logical and not, she shouted to Natalie,

'Nat, Nat, come down here. Quick,' as she hovered in the doorway between the lounge and the stairs. She heard the bed creak, followed by Natalie's surprised gasp of 'what the hell'

They met at the bottom of the stairs, Lisa looking puzzled and Natalie looking worried, as she shot out a quick 'what's wrong, What is it, are you ok?' Lisa nodded she was fine, and took Natalie's hand to lead her into the lounge, as she explained 'the front door was open when I came downstairs, it's ok, there's no one here' she quickly reassured, as she saw Natalie's eyes darting around in fear 'but look' she pointed at the picture hanging on the wall. Natalie looked at Lisa questioningly, then grinned.

'Is this a joke, like someone would break into our house to hang a picture on the wall, ha-ha, you could have just said you bought a painting'.

'No, babe, that's just it. I didn't buy a painting. The door really was open. I've never seen this painting before. Well, I've seen the original it's hanging in the Louvre. Who couldn't know the Mona Lisa when they saw her.'

Lisa's voice trailed off as her eyes moved from Natalie's face, to Natalie's feet, to the painting and the open door. Then back to Natalie.

'Natalie, look at your feet.' Natalie looked down to her feet, as Lisa whispered, 'oh my god Nat! Your feet are filthy. It's you, you've been out walking again. Please tell me that's not the original,' she cried as the sound of sirens drowned out her question.

SLEEPWALKING

April Berry

Patrick returned from the clinic. He felt refreshed and at ease with the world, a feeling he had not had for a long time. The last 6 months had been hell. He'd lost his job. His mother-in-law had custody of his two children because he had lost the family home, and could only afford a one bed flat. He only got to see them every two weeks, which he relished. All this tragedy was the fallout from the killing of his wife in a horrendous attack one night. That the killer hadn't meant to do it, that it was an accident, didn't make the hurt any better, nor did it do anything to quash the rising anger in Patrick, which seemed to get worse with every passing day.

Unlocking the door, Patrick picked up his post, threw it on the kitchen counter and made himself a coffee. Taking leaflets about the clinic from his pocket and putting them with the post, Patrick took his drink, and went upstairs. He was shattered; he found it extremely difficult to sleep at the clinic. Last night was the eighth night he had been there. Only two more to go, he thought to himself. But it was worth every sleepless minute.

Making plans in his head for the rest of the day. His priority was a new job, so he needed to update and register his CV on job websites, but first he needed a shower and a quick nap. Patrick switched on the shower and radio, stripped off and stepped in to wash the clinical smells off his body.

A loud banging on his flat door drowned out the dulcet tones of Paloma Faith enticing him to New York. Patrick quickly rinsed off when it became apparent the banging wasn't stopping. Stepping out of the shower, he picked up a towel, trying to wrap it round himself whilst opening the door at the same time. Facing Patrick on the doorstep was the detective in charge of the investigation into his wife's murder. Patrick had spent hours with the detective, but something told Patrick today's visit wasn't a friendly one.

Before he knew what was happening, Patrick found himself handcuffed and in the back of a police car, arrested on suspicion of murder. Patrick was shell-shocked! What was happening?

Will his nightmares never end?

At the police station Patrick was fingerprinted, handcuffed, and taken into a square, gloomy interview room and sat down at a table. The officer had given him the right to a solicitor, so Patrick was waiting for her to arrive before he would say anything to the officers across the table.

Julia, his solicitor, walked in the door and immediately commanded Patrick not to say a word. She demanded to know why Patrick was under arrest, what he had done, and what evidence the police had to support the arrest.

Patrick was astounded as the police laid out the sequence of events as they saw them. They had accused him of attacking Sean Williams and killing him; the police had CCTV footage and an eyewitness who had named him because of the extensive TV coverage around his wife's murder. Patrick couldn't believe what was happening to him. A doctor examined him to look for any marks that he may have sustained during the attack. His flat, according to his solicitor, had been torn apart.

He hated his cellmate and argued with him every day he was in prison awaiting his trial.

Eventually, four months after being arrested, Patrick was in court. The hearing lasted ten days, with expert witnesses on either side, the defence specialists putting the mitigation to the jury and the prosecution specialists arguing against any mitigation.

The crucial evidence that worked in Patrick's favour and the eventual Not Guilty verdict were the leaflets from the clinic that he had carelessly thrown on the kitchen units with his post the last day he had been in his flat.

After all, if Sean Williams could get away with murdering Patrick's wife by claiming he was sleepwalking when he did it, so could Patrick!

SUMMER HOLIDAY

Jayne Love

Lady Alice Grainger strolled along the promenade for the first time in forty-nine years, feeling a little sentimental about her life. She'd married well, to a kind military man. They had two wonderful children, Miles Jr. and Ada-May. She had even dined with royalty in her time.

Miles Sr. was a good man. She cared deeply for him and spent her life doting on the children. She laughed as she thought of the daft things her son did as a boy and how sad she was when he was shipped off to military school, but he loved it. He was so like his father; she thought. A smile formed on her lips as she reminisced. She loved her children dearly.

Ada-May was like her dad too, but could not join the military. She'd refused to marry any of the three men her father deemed suitable. 'Stubborn as they come, that one,' he'd said 'don't know where she gets it from.' He'd laughed as he looked at Alice.

Miles Sr. had died almost five years ago of a heart attack, and Alice still missed him. His passing was a shock, as he was seldom ill. He may not have been the love of her life, but he was her best friend and they had many happy years together.

Alice sat on a bench watching young lovers walking hand in hand, laughing together, and stopping for the occasional kiss. Then she noticed two girls holding hands. Her mind wandered back forty-nine years to when she first met Ada, a striking looking dark-haired lass of eighteen. She had the most beautiful blue eyes and an infectious laugh. Within two weeks of meeting her, Alice spent every waking moment thinking of her, which was very confusing, as this just wasn't the way one thought about girls! She wondered what had become of her friend after they parted on Blackpool train station all those years ago.

Alice was a little cold. She absentmindedly pulled her coat around herself as her mind wandered back in time. Her life had been all mapped out for her. It was the last holiday she'd take with her parents. Next year she'd be twenty-one, and married to Miles. She would have a large house, staff to manage, and children to bear. However, before all of that, there was Ada.

She wasn't sure how the relationship developed so quickly. Maybe it was Adas' contagious zest for life, the way she'd grasped every moment with both hands. She was an intelligent girl full of ideas and aspirations. She remembered wondering if Ada could ever live life on her own terms, which was almost unthinkable back then.

Alice recalls one afternoon about an hour after lunch asking Ada what she would like to do. 'Let's get changed and go to *The Tower* for tea,' Ada replied. The two had gone up to Alice's room and, as Alice undressed, she noticed Ada watching her. At first she was shocked but slowly realised she liked her watching. She smiled as her friend came closer. 'Alice, you're so beautiful,' Ada whispered. Alice blushed, and Ada touched her face gently. 'I want to kiss you,' Ada said. Alice had surprised herself by leaning forward and pressing her lips on Ada's.

The two girls stopped for a moment to look at one another before kissing once more with growing passion. They drew each other closer and undid their clothes. The feelings were overwhelming, like a fire burning within them. Then the most amazing feeling ran through Alice, throughout her body, right down to her toes, like nothing she'd ever known before. When Ada achieved the same feeling, the two girls lay on the bed and giggled.

Over the next few days, they explored each other more, taking each other to new heights, growing closer and closer.

On the last day of their holiday, the thought dawned that the next time they met, they would probably be with their husbands. They hugged as Alice boarded the train, with promises of writing to each other, staying in touch. But as is often the case, life got in the way. Alice had never got back to Blackpool. Holidays were abroad with Miles, usually for work. She wondered if Ada ever returned. Did she ever think about that summer when they touched each other's hearts so intimately? Alice felt a little sad.

'Alice, Alice, is that you, lass?' A voice from behind her was calling, 'Come on lass, let's go swimming.' Alice laughed to herself. She closed her eyes. She could see Ada in a blue costume with white edges on the skirt. 'Don't wear the hat' Alice's memory said, 'I like the way your hair clings to you when it's wet.' She smiled at the memory.

'Alice, Alice,' the voice again, persistent, she turned to see a woman waving to her. 'I knew it was you,' the woman said. The two ladies looked at each other and they hugged. 'Least we won't get arrested for this now days,' the woman said as she laughed. No mistaking that laugh, Alice thought.

'Ada, what are you doing here?' Alice said.

'Waiting for you, my love,' she replied.

Alice smiled. 'I have thought about you so often, Ada,' she said. 'Why did you stop writing? I called my daughter Ada-May after you. I missed you, every day I thought of you.' All the words came flooding out of Alice in a rush.

Ada just smiled at her friend. 'I know,' she whispered. 'Shall we walk along the beach?'

'Yes, that will be lovely, but I don't walk so well these days' Alice replied.

'We could dance if you wish,' Ada laughed.

The next day the headline read: Lady Alice Grainger died in Blackpool, aged seventy. Pictured here with her companion Ms. Ada-May Simpson, who died in 1944. Shot dead by firing squad for sheltering Jews in France. Both women holidayed in Blackpool.

SUMMER HOLIDAY

Dean Wrigley

It was Michael's final full day of his holiday. His flight home was early the next morning. This time tomorrow he'd be back in the UK and back at work the day after that. All things must pass.

He had had a lie-in today and had been very late to breakfast, so he rounded it all off with a PIMMS No. 1 while sitting outside wearing shades with the sun high in the clear blue sky.

One of this morning's new arrivals caught his eye. She was skipping down the steps wearing a very short crop-top with no bra underneath. With every step, her nipples played peek-a-boo with him. He smiled as she glanced in his direction before walking through the reception area.

Moments later, she came charging back through, up the steps, and disappeared. A few minutes after that she came hurrying down the steps again, with a bearded man just behind her in hot pursuit. She lost her footing on a step and almost tumbled over, but the man grabbed her so high around her torso that he took partial hold of her breasts as he stopped her from slipping down any further. She gathered herself and steadied her feet. They both roared with laughter and then they were both off again, running through reception to the road outside.

Out by the bus stop, a woman was waiting for her husband and her sister to return. "Trust you two to forget your passports," she complained. 'And if you're going to wear that top, put a bra on too, you brazen hussy! Too late, here's the bus. Oh well, here we go again.'

'Look, Trish. I'll wear what I want to wear and how I want to wear it. I'm on holiday and I'm not bothered about some creepy guy staring and smiling at me.'

They spent the afternoon wandering around the market stalls in the town. Ginny spent most of her time sorting through some pretty cotton dresses. She preferred the long, airy ones that would keep her cool while affording some protection from the glare of the sun. Also, she could be naked underneath and her older sister couldn't have any complaints about it; she haggled for two.

They ate in the town and caught the late bus back to their hotel. Trish and her husband, Glenn, were tired from the heat and the walking, so they went to bed. Refreshed and changed, Ginny had a couple of drinks in the hotel bar.

Michael noticed her disappear into the crowd at the bar and emerge minutes later and take a table outside on her own. He walked over to her and asked what she was doing alone.

Ginny looked up and saw a handsome man dressed in chinos and a shirt. 'My sister and brother-in-law have gone to bed, but I thought I'd have a nightcap before I turn in.'

'May I join you?' he asked. 'I'm Michael, by the way.'

She motioned a welcome to him joining her at the table, 'Hello Michael, I'm Virginia but friends call me Ginny.'

Conversation between them flowed. There was shared laughter and a connection. There were stories and beliefs. There was chemistry and magic. She was so comfortable with his company that when he suggested a walk around the little park near the harbour opposite the hotel; she didn't hesitate, even though it was well past midnight.

They sat on a bench and turned towards each other. Michael unbuttoned his shirt, slipped it off, and allowed it to drop behind him. Ginny laughed and touched his chest.

'I suppose you expect me to take my top off now,' she joked.

'Do whatever you like. It's still so hot,' he said. The conversation flowed. They were alone.

He noticed her look over his shoulder. She looked across the park and all around her. There was no one to be seen.

Grabbing the hem of her top, she pulled it up and off over her head and placed it on the bench behind her. She looked deep into his eyes as they sat facing each other topless. He lifted his hand and touched her breast, running his fingers down to circle and gently squeeze the nipple. He moved his hand lower and ran his fingers up the side of her abdomen. She was thrilled at his touch and pulled him towards her. Their chests and their lips met and the rush through their bodies was palpable. She lifted her face as he kissed down her throat.

Suddenly, she felt cold. Not from the air, but towards a situation she could so easily fall into again. She pulled away from him, reached around for her top, pulled it back down over her body, and stood up.

'I came on holiday to enjoy myself, not to have my heart broken again. Sorry Michael, I have to go. Thank you for a lovely evening. Have a safe journey home tomorrow and enjoy the rest of your life.' And with that, she was gone.

Two years later Michael is travelling East. His daughter had recently graduated and found herself a job in The East Midlands and a place to live for a while as she settled into her new environment.

'I live in a really friendly area, Dad, and my landlady is adorable. I know you'll love her. Everybody loves Ginny.'

There was a name that brought back memories. Wonderful memories. Michael gave himself the privilege of reminiscing for a few moments before shaking his head and laughing. 'Don't be silly,' he said to himself. 'She lives on the south coast. It wouldn't be my Ginny. Not the one that got away. Not in a million years. Ha ha! How crazy would that be?'

He pulled his car up outside the house. Took some of his daughter's belongings from the boot and walked up the garden path. He pressed the doorbell and heard footsteps getting closer. The latch turned, the door opened, and the craziness began.

SUMMER HOLIDAY

Carolyn Ward-Daniels

The sun was on Olga's shoulders as she stood on the promenade. Her shadow was tall, stretched out on the dimpled sand. The beach was empty, the tide way out and she stared at it, knowing it was there she became a widow, and something else, but she had come to terms with both.

She smiled at her slim shadow being seven stone lighter than that summer holiday in '77, and it was exactly seven years ago. Maybe seven should be my lucky number, she thought. This was the first time she had been back since that fateful day.

In 1970 she was a 20-year-old miserable virgin living in a grand house in London with her father, a Russian diplomat, and her browbeaten mother. That autumn, the boiler refused to work and a plumbing company had to be brought in. Bob Sharp, who knew the archaic system, took his assistant Steve with him. Steve was a good worker because Steve liked money. He was saving for a flash motor. When Bob stopped outside the house, Steve whistled, 'This is a bit posh, ain't it.'

'Yeah, behave yourself in there, keep your 'ead dahn, get the job done.'

Inside was faded opulence, but grand. There were staff everywhere and an overbearing feeling of being watched. The heating system had to be drained, which meant visiting every room. In one bedroom, Steve couldn't help but hear English gossip. Out in the corridors it was all foreign words. Two girls making a bed were whispering, but he could hear.

'That daughter never goes out.'

'Is she allowed?'

'Surely. I mean, she has no siblings. You'd think she'd want to get away from that lot out there.'

'She always looks so sad.'

A stern bloke on the landing escorted Steve to each door. He was having trouble with a radiator valve when the bedroom door opened and in walked a sad looking young woman. Steve said 'Sorry, the chap let me in, got to.'

'I know, tis all right' came the accented reply. She picked a book up from the bedside and left. He fantasised about getting off with this daughter. She was no beauty but not ugly either, and the only offspring of this rich family. She could be the heiress to a fortune. He made sure he crossed paths with her several times, making excuses to go back into a room he'd found her in.

Steve was a good-looking charmer, and he got the sad girl smiling. The plumbing job was going to take several visits as the parts were special order. So Steve made it his job to go after the rich Russian girl. After just six months of courting and a couple of uncomfortable family dinners, he decided he would dare ask her stone faced father for her hand in marriage. He expected a definite no. There was no change in emotion from the man, even the mother was blank of face. All Olga's father asked was 'Are you able to take care of her, do you have means?'

Now Steve had gone the extra mile and used his savings to buy an impressive diamond engagement ring. It was bloody expensive, but he thought the investment would be well worth it. He got giddy every time he went to the house with its huge paintings and elaborate silverware. When he slid the ring on Olga's finger, she was so happy. It was too big, but she didn't care. She had fallen in love with this good-looking Englishman and at last she felt she belonged.

Two months later Olga fell pregnant, and the wedding had to be rushed. Steve thought they would want a lavish affair but was relieved when they quickly organised a registrar wedding and it was over. He was pleased because he didn't want his friends to see his plain, frumpy bride. Much to Steve's dismay, they were given a dowdy little flat to rent. He couldn't believe they weren't allowed to live in the big house. He had looked forward to pulling up outside, showing off that he lived there. Then something went haywire. The British government was expelling Russian diplomats for being spies and it devastated Steve that the grand house didn't belong to Olga's parents and, back in Russia, they had a rented apartment.

Olga could now stay in Britain and didn't lose any love when her parents shipped out. She miscarried and it upset both of them even though Steve didn't think he was ready for kids, especially with a poor, plain Russian girl. However, two years later she was pregnant again and went the full term only for their baby to be stillborn. Olga was beyond devastated and cried nonstop and ate with grief and piled on the fat. Steve became bitter and hostile, calling her lard arse and pulling faces of disgust at her. She was without a family to run to and couldn't put the loss of her baby girl out of her mind.

She was quite obese when they went on their first summer holiday, but she braved putting on a bathing costume and waddled after Steve down to the sea. All the way down the beach, he verbally attacked her. 'Don't fall over, you'll look like a beached whale and I can't pick you up.' She was used to it and hated him for it. One time he asked for her engagement ring back so he could sell it, saying it cost him a fortune and she wasn't worth it. She refused.

Steve was wading into the waves. 'C'mon you fat cow,' he yelled. She despised him.

He made her life completely miserable. She slipped off the engagement ring and tucked it up into her tight costume. 'Oh no! The ring has come off!'

'What! you stupid bitch.' He splashed back to her, 'Where?'

'Here, somewhere.'

He flopped down in the water feeling the sand and Olga flopped down on top of him.

SUMMER HOLIDAY

April Berry

Stood in her Kitchen, Amy was daydreaming, a rare quiet moment in the hustle and bustle of returning from holiday.

As a child, she'd loved summer holidays, all the preparation and anticipation in the buildup to going away. Packing her suitcase with all the new clothes that her parents had bought, especially for the holiday. Amy also always made sure that Teddy, her stuffed panda, was included in her luggage and enough books for the week.

She wasn't keen on the journey to and from the coast, having to sit in the back of the car with her little brother, so a book would take her mind off his tormenting and whining, 'are we there yet, Dad.' Her family spent most of their summer holidays on the Yorkshire coast, normally Bridlington, sometimes Whitby, which was Amy's favourite place with its quaint harbour, cliffs, and rock pools to explore.

Dragging herself back to the present, she sighed. It didn't appear to be this hectic when she was a child. She heard her partner Jeremy returning with the children. They looked worn out and sad. Amy assumed it was that they were missing the fun that they had all experienced on their recent holiday.

Two weeks on Crete, a fabulous Greek island, with white sands, that in certain lights appeared to have a pink hue about them. The beautiful shallow lagoon, perfect for the children to bathe in, although they were both splendid swimmers, something that her partner had insisted on, possibly because that was something Jeremy couldn't do, and he was too stubborn to have lessons. That was about the only thing that Amy found lacking in Jeremy. Everything else was, well, if not perfect, about as near perfection as one person could get.

As she watched Jeremy and the children emptying suitcases, putting the laundry into piles to do the massive amount of washing that always followed a holiday, she smiled to herself and in her mind transported herself back to the Island.

Beaches that were secluded in the morning, heavenly waters, and, if you were lucky, you could see seals and sea turtles playing in the ocean.

Both she and Jeremy had demanding jobs, made worse by the pandemic. Holiday's last year were non-existent, all 4 of them cooped up in the house 24/7. Amy and Jeremy working from home, home schooling the children, on a roller coaster of emotions for over twelve months. Frustration, anxiety, worry encroaching on what had been up to now quite a calm life for all the family. So the first chance they got to get away, Amy grabbed it with both hands.

For Amy, it had been the perfect holiday. The children hadn't squabbled at all. They had stayed in an Idyllic hotel, hired a car and explored. The perfect mix of rest, sightseeing and activity, who could want for more.

Bringing herself back to the present, she could see Jeremy with his arms round the children, hugging them tight to him and was whispering something to them that Amy couldn't make out. Amy loved how Jeremy was with the children, and she commented as much to him.

Jeremy did not hear Amy speaking to him, though. He was too busy comforting the children, and trying as hard as he could to stop himself from crying. All the time cursing himself for his stubbornness in not learning to swim, because if he had, he would have been able to save Amy from drowning when she got into difficulties snorkelling in that beautiful lagoon.

SUMMER HOLIDAY

Daizi Rae

Jess sat out on the deck of the chalet she had rented for the week at Scarborough, with a well-earned glass of Lambrusco, which her budget just about stretched to. She was a single parent working a call centre job, a modern day factory if ever there was one, but it paid the bills. A rogue tear rolled down her cheek that she didn't bother to wipe away. Why should she? Once a year on this date, she treated herself to a bottle of wine, always Lambrusco, as that was their bottle of choice as teenagers. She sat and lamented the loss of her love and mourned the future they would never have. The memories came flooding back, as clear as if it had been yesterday.

Jess had been on the last summer holiday that she would ever take with her parents. The sun had shone the entire week; the sea was warm, and the fun fair was in town. It was glorious. Jess was seventeen, only two months off her eighteenth birthday, and feeling every bit the young adult, she was positively glowing that summer.

She met Sam on the funfair, mucky blonde hair and a twinkle in his amber eyes. Jess thought he was the most handsome lad she'd ever seen. He was working on the haunted house with his dad, Brian, just as he'd done before him, with Sam's grandad, a real family affair. He would stand inside the ride and whenever a car of punters rattled past him, he would jump out and frighten the life out of them. He enjoyed it; it was a fun way to spend time with his family before he was due to go off to university in the autumn.

He was standing in the shadows, ready to leap out at the next car on the ride, grinning to himself. Some of the faces they pulled when he frightened them had him crying, laughing. It was a hell of a way to make a living. Jess was sitting in that car, prepared to be scared, but smiling all the same. Sam leapt, locked eyes with Jess, and fell. Instantly smitten.

They were inseparable from that day on. The summer of love may be a bit of a cliché, but it was as true for Jess and Sam that summer as it was for any of the great love stories that inspired it. From the innocence of awkward walks on the beach, anticipating the first kiss. To tentative lovemaking. Through to an all-consuming passion and making plans for their future together. However, as with all the great love stories across time from Romeo and Juliet to Jack and Rose, its death that brings a tragic end to their love story, too.

Sam's dad, Brian, had stood before Jess, a broken man. Trying and failing to speak the words aloud to explain how one mistimed leap inside the Haunted House had taken his son from him. It was devastating. She wouldn't have got through the rest of that summer without her mum and dad and their constant support. She didn't want to carry on. What was the point without Sam? But her mum made her food every day for weeks that she couldn't eat. She was so sick with grief. Until she did, and little by little she came to realise that life would carry on, that Sam hadn't left her all alone after all. She didn't know it then, but come Christmas, her oh so loving, supportive mum would have thrown her out of the only home she'd ever known, while her dad stood mute.

They hadn't spoken in nine years now. In the beginning, Jess had been crushed, and had spent the longest time waiting for a knock at the door. How could they not want to know their grandson? But time went on and the knock on the door never came. Eventually, Jess stopped waiting and learned to live life on her own terms. Did she really want to forgive her parents for punishing an innocent?

Matty was eight now, and Jess's world. He was so like his dad, right down to the mucky blonde hair and amber eyes. Just as she was thinking of Matty, he came tearing out onto the deck. 'Mum, mum, I heard the music from the funfair. Can we go? Please mum, can we? I'm big enough now.'

Despite herself, Jess smiled at him as she replied, 'If you get yourself off to bed and go straight to sleep, I guess we can go tomorrow.'

Matty kissed his mum loudly on the cheek and hugged her hard, grinning from ear to ear 'Yeah! Thanks mum, I'll go straight to sleep, I promise.' And as quick as he'd appeared, he'd gone again.

After they'd been on the fair for about half an hour, Matty

caught sight of the Haunted House. He stared at it, enthralled. 'Wow, look mum, can I go on there, please. Please let me.'

As Jess looked over, she saw Brian was still working on the ride. She caught his eye and a huge grin lit up his face as he saw her.

'Jess! How wonderful to see you.'

His arms opened wide to embrace her in a bear hug, but he stopped dead in his tracks when he saw Matty standing beside her. It was like looking at eight-year-old Sam. Brian was stunned.

'Oh Jess, why didn't you tell me?'

Matty went on the Haunted House while his mum and Brian talked and hugged, and talked some more. When the ride finished Matty got off and ran to his mum, saying, 'Mum, mum, the ghosts on this haunted house aren't scary at all. One of them even sat in my car with me and gave me a cuddle.'

Brian and Jess looked at Matty astounded, and Brian threw his arms around them both as he said, 'it's time you two came home.'

THE SCAM

Gerry O'Keeffe

Mother sat at the dinner table tucking into her favourite chunky crispy chips, covered in golden yellow yoke from her fried egg, listening to her twins Tracy & Tom, both mad into computer games, discussing the latest state-of-the-art virtual reality game. They were excited about its daring escape rooms, with all kinds of puzzles to solve, with fire and falling debris to add to the drama when the game became time critical.

'The High Definition makes it as real as you could get too' Said Tracy.

'Especially when deep sea diving, or on archaeological digs or jungle expeditions.' Tom replied excitedly.

Their father wasn't in the picture. He had left when they were still babies, so mother compensated by spoiling them rotten. Which they took full advantage of regularly. You could even say they scammed their mother by pretending to get into scrapes and fights or so-called accidents. Tracy had been studying movie make-up and could create quite impressive fake cuts and bruises. While Tom learnt how to fall off bikes or ladders etc…, or even trip over objects without actually hurting himself. They were a great double act. They could make it in show business someday. They had a birthday coming up, and they knew if they talked the new game up where mother could overhear, she'd think it was a great idea. And just as expected, there she was, listening to every word. This was perfect, so they put the next part of their devious plan into action to claim their biggest prize yet.

While eating their egg and chips, they both curled up in pain, groaning right on cue, and then raced out of the room. Tracy to the upstairs bathroom and Tom to the downstairs loo. With both doors quickly locked, horrible noises began reverberating throughout the entire house.

Mother sat horrified, yoke covered chip hovering by her mouth. She dropped her fork, thinking she had poisoned them, and pushed her plate away. When the noises finally stopped and

Tracy and Tom staggered out of their respective bathrooms, mother fussed over them, hugging them tightly, apologising profusely, and promising to make it up to them. The terrible twins had beaming smiles on their faces, hidden behind their mother's hugs, knowing their plan had worked.

On the morning of the twins birthday, they excitedly ran downstairs, ignoring the huge 'HAPPY BIRTHDAY' banner and balloons that decorated the walls of the staircase, to find an enormous bow across the spare room door doorway. Mother was standing outside the door holding a pair of scissors to cut the ribbon to their birthday surprise. With bated breath and bubbling excitement, they cut the ribbon and opened the door, to discover a room full of magic and wonder. They could see steps to climb, tunnels to crawl through, a raised pool that could create water effects, a treasure chest filled with sweets and other treasures to search through. There were doorways to open with combination locks to solve, and in the middle of the room was a sofa equipped with all the latest games tech, remote controls and virtual reality headsets and all facing a painted white wall their new games could be projected onto. As well as all this, there was a cabinet containing all the latest games consoles and the brand new game they had scammed their mother for. They hugged her so tight, they couldn't believe they had pulled this off.

Over the next few weeks and months, they enjoyed their new games room. Playing each new game, solving each hurdle and adventure along the way. Moving gleefully onto each new challenge with grit and determination, finding them harder and more physically demanding every time. They were feeling happily exhausted at the end of each gaming session, and a little guilty, too, because after an afternoon of gaming, they'd leave their room in a complete mess and go back to find it all clean and tidy. Or after dinner, they'd finish their game to find the kitchen all cleaned up. Another afternoon, they'd look out of the window to find the gardening all done, too.

'Mother must do all this work on her own, while we have all this fun,' Tracy said to Tom, feeling guilty.

Then one morning while she was on a treasure hunt with a metal detector and finding gold, Tracy, in her excitement, knocked off her virtual reality headset to find. In fact, she was vacuuming the living room floor. She looked over at Tom, who thought he was looking for ancient artefacts, to see he was dusting and tidying the mantelpiece. Tracy stopped him. Reality dawned as they stood round-eyed, looking at one another. In unison they yelled, 'Mother!' realising they were the ones being scammed now.

She entered the room, smiling. Having been aware of their scams all along, she'd plotted a way to exact revenge, have some fun, and teach them a lesson in the process. They followed her back to the games room, where she showed them her tricks.

The two escape room doors lead to the kitchen and the garden. The pool had a soapsuds dispenser in it where they'd been washing the dishes. The steps and tunnels led to a hatch into their bedroom. Everything was rigged, set up to get all the housework done while mother sat with her feet up, playing on her games, 'pile up the dishes,' and 'make my garden beautiful' How ironic was that? But that wasn't the only surprise. Oh, no.

Mother had invented all these games and didn't need to work any more. But by far the best thing of all for her, as the twins stood there in shock, mouths hanging open, was the joy of scamming the scammers.

THE SCAM

Daizi Rae

It is said that Karma refers to the spiritual principle of cause and effect, where the intent and actions of a person directly influences their future: good intent and good deeds contribute to good karma and happier rebirths, while bad intent and bad deeds, well, let's just see where that goes.

Let me introduce John. On some deep, almost forgotten level, John believes in karma. Or he used to, before it was more convenient to forget it. As a child, he'd grown up with it being a big part of his family's beliefs and it always made a kind of perfect sense to him. As a still relatively young thirty-six year old, those philosophies he'd grown up with had slipped his mind somewhere along the line.

We can find John sitting in his favourite blood red chesterfield armchair, his feet propped up on a matching footstool, with a warm tartan throw over his legs, to keep off the autumn chill. Despite the heat emanating from the open fire, John feels the cold running right through to his bones, but honestly, that's probably more about his current state of mind. You see, he's just received a call from his doctor, with the kind of news no one ever wants to hear, and it's triggering a worrying chain of thought.

When he'd been in school, he'd had a solid belief in rebirth, every living beings soul sort of recycling after death, carrying the seeds of karmic impulses from the life just completed, into the next life, and the next one, indefinitely. The realisation of what John has done to his own future over the last decade has just hit him like a sledgehammer.

Several years ago now, John and his then wife Deborah had convinced thousands of people all over the United Kingdom that local landed gentry Lady Elizabeth Coates had died. Leaving a substantial estate with no will or next of kin to inherit her fortunes. They had contacted all the people named Coates they could find in the UK. The story they told them was that they represented Lady Elizabeth's estate, and they would stake a claim on the late heiresses estate in their name, for the comparatively small fee of just five thousand pounds. A mere drop in the ocean compared to their possible future wealth.

Around three thousand unfortunates named Coates had been gullible enough, or greedy enough, as John had believed, to part with their hard-earned money. They had practically been queueing up to give their money away to John and Deborah. It was such an easy lie to sell. The Coates family name was a noble one of English heritage on the Staffordshire borders. A family so private that no one really knew the actual story behind their lives or their wealth.

John and Deborah had quietly run this scam over several years, until they had bought the house of their dreams, and had sufficient money to live the life they'd wished to become accustomed to.

John now sat trying to wrap his already muddy, and preoccupied, mind around potentially fixing the wicked deeds it had taken him years to execute. It seemed to be an impossible task, one akin to swimming through treacle, as his granny used to say.

Attempting to make amends or reparation to atone for ones sins requires remorse, a belief of wrong doing. Not an egocentric, self-absorbed need to buy oneself a comfortable time in the next life.

Karma is creating havoc with what is left of Johns future in this life, as well as his future lives. The next three thousand of which he has every right to be worried about.

DIRTY WEEKEND

Carolyn Ward-Daniels

Leo was lying on his bed, checking his phone for any sign of life outside of his bedroom. He was bored and needed some excitement in his life. He was old enough to go drinking, and the pubs had reopened, but he was skint. There was a knock on his door followed by his mother's tired voice calling in a questioning tone, 'Leo?'

'Yeah.'

'I'm off cleaning now. I want you to take the bag of clean laundry to Aunty Kath.'

'Aww Mam.'

This response made Pat open the door and show her angry face. 'Too busy are yer?'

'I've got to sign on at 10.'

'That's worked out well. Yer Aunty is just round the corner from there.'

'Can't our Phil teck it, he's gorra car.'

'He's also got a job and a family. And don't empty the fridge. I don't get paid for two days. Now get up and make yerself useful. The lawn needs cutting, yer nineteen not twelve!'

Pat left the door open as if it would encourage the idleness to escape.

Kath gave him three quid, so he called at the chippy. The girl who worked behind the counter was Kirsty Parker, and Leo fancied her like crazy. He even blushed slightly if their hands touched when he paid his money. He took his food over to the park to eat, as he was aware that his eating style was on the ugly side. His mother reminded him regularly, and he didn't want Kirsty to see him ram a battered sausage in. The more he thought about Kirsty, the less he wanted his chips and threw them in the bin. He sat there on a bench just staring down the park. He looked to his left and saw Kirsty leaving the chippy. She was in running gear. Then a car pulled up, and a girl got out, also in Lycra shorts and vest. They both looked at their watches and then started jogging toward the park. Leo felt like Billy no mates so took out his phone, turned to the side and pretended to be talking to someone as they passed. They were breathlessly talking and laughing and what Leo heard made him upset and he wished he hadn't chucked his chips.

Leo wasted away the afternoon avoiding home as he knew there were chores he should do. He sauntered to his brother's house for 6 and saw his car on the drive. He could hear his young nieces play screaming in the back garden. His brother Phil answered the door.

'Hello Bro, come on in what you doing here?'

'Just fed up.' Leo was jealous of his brother. The house was always a happy zone, his wife Pam was lovely, and the girls adored their daddy and the fridge was always full.

'Hiya Pam.'

'Hello love, what's up? Lost your smile?'

'Not much to smile about.'

Phil asked if he'd found a job. Leo scratched his unruly blonde head and pulled a face. 'No jobs about.'

'Try looking a bit harder.' Phil said. He loved his brother, but not his lack of trying.

Pam was cooking and sipping wine. Phil got Leo a bottle of beer and wanted to know why Leo was down.

'Oh, it's just this girl I fancy. Seems like she's got a boyfriend.'

'Anyone I know?'

'Kirsty Parker, works at the chippy.'

Pam said, 'Oh, my sister's friend, who's the boyfriend?'

'Dunno.'

'Well, how do you know she's got one?' Phil asked.

'Heard her talkin' to her mate on about going running with a fella on a dirty weekend.'

There was a laugh from Pam. Phil and Leo looked at her.

'Is that what she said?'

'Well, they were running passed me quite close, I was on me phone.'

Pam laughed again, 'Oh Leo, Kirsty and Lisa go Fell running, they're training for the Peak event. They call it the dirty weekend because they get covered in mud!'

Leo grinned and Phil laughed, 'You knob.'

Two days later, Leo rang his brother. 'I've done it! I've got a date with Kirsty.'

Phil couldn't quite believe it and said 'Really?'

'Yep, we already had a small date, just a coffee this afternoon and we are going out for a drink. Oh, she is so fit. Phil, have you got any jobs I could do this weekend to earn a few quid to take her out?'

'You could polish my car and mow the lawns.'

While Leo polished the car, Phil taunted him about his date. 'I can't believe you pulled Kirsty, punching above your weight there.'

'Ha, well, you did alright with the lovely Pam and you're no George Clooney. How did you manage that?'

'Charmed her.'

Leo stopped now and looked serious. 'I could do with a few tips. I've never been on a proper date before and I really like her. How did you charm Pam?'

'To be honest, I looked a bit of poetry up, memorised a few lines.'

'Like what?'

'Err... I said something like. 'Your beauty stems the hands of time. When I look into your eyes, time stands still.'

'Wow.'

When Leo phoned Phil next, he sounded miserable.

'What's up? How did the date go?'

'I don't know what went wrong.'

'What happened?'

'It was going great. We had a couple of drinks and were having a laugh and then I ran out of words and felt a bit nervous. I am so crazy about her and didn't want to lose her, so I remembered what you said. I made myself all serious like and lowered my voice and said what you said.'

'What did you say, Leo?'

'I said, all romantic like, Kirsty, you have the kind of face that would stop a clock. Then she slammed her drink down and stormed off!'

'Oh Leo, you knob.'

DIRTY WEEKEND

Daizi Rae

Maggie woke up with the onset of a hangover. She opened her eyes, not recognising the room she was in. It took a second to realise she was in Mark's bed, and not at home at all. The images of last night came flooding back. It was the first time she'd stayed at Marks since they started dating six months ago. A grin lit up her face as she gave a contented little sigh.

She wasn't sure whether to wait for Mark to come back to bed or just go join him out in the kitchen. Then she realised she could hear him talking on the phone. She didn't want to interrupt, so she headed to the bathroom to clean her teeth. She definitely didn't want morning breath when he came back to bed. As she turned to close the bathroom door, she realised the acoustics in the bathroom meant she could now hear his conversation clearly. She headed for the sink to turn on the tap to mute his conversation, but before she got there, she inadvertently caught the tail end of his conversation.

'… so I'm going to take her away for the weekend. It'll be really dirty, I'll let you know how it goes. Oh I definitely think she'll be surprised' she heard Mark say with a chuckle. 'See you matey.'

Maggie uttered a disappointed and confused 'oh!' On automatic pilot, she turned on the tap and cleaned her teeth. Her mind was whirring ten to the dozen. Did he think she was easy? Was he being offensive, or complementary? No, no, it was definitely offensive. A dirty weekend implied she was some kind of sex object, and he was bragging on the phone about it. What the hell! She left the bathroom and got dressed before heading into the kitchen to join Mark. He looked up from buttering toast and his eyes widened as he saw she was dressed and ready to leave.

'Oh, you're up, is everything ok Maggie? I was just making us some breakfast.'

He sounded genuinely concerned, which confused Maggie a little, but she remained firm and made her excuses to leave, muttering something about an unexpected work call, as she hurried out of the door.

As Maggie made her way to the tram stop, she didn't know if she was more upset or angry. Bloody men! She called her best friend Julie. Julie was her most practical friend and the bluntest. She could always count on her for an honest opinion. When she'd done explaining, there was silence on the call for a minute while Julie digested everything before giving her considered opinion.

'So you've been together six months right, and he's never acted this way before?'

'No, never. That's why I thought we were ready to take it to the next level. He's put no pressure on me, and staying over last night, that was my idea really.'

'Ok' Julie said 'so playing devil's advocate, this is what I think could be happening. First, he really likes you, and the mate he was talking to this morning was taking the piss, and Mark felt like he had to respond in kind, so he didn't look soft in front of him.'

'Ok, maybe,' Maggie conceded, before Julie continued.

'Second, maybe what you heard was out of context. There could have been some much more complimentary stuff said before you fell into the conversation. Or third, it wasn't about you at all.'

'What!' Maggie squeaked.

'Ok, ok, so lastly then, it's a massive compliment that he thinks you're so incredible after spending one night with you he wants to whisk you away for the weekend. He's just got a crappy turn of phrase. Maybe you should just enjoy the moment.'

Maggie leaves things as they are for a few days to think. She likes Mark. Could she be mistaken?

When Mark calls to ask her if she'd like to go away for the weekend, at the end of the month, he seemed surprisingly nervous. But Maggie didn't think about that, she just agreed to go. No questions asked.

The next week is a flurry of plucking, waxing, manicure, pedicure, hairdressers, new lingerie, and new clothes. The pièce de résistance being the sexiest of all nightgowns. She spent a fortune. If she was going to do this, she was out to impress.

When Mark arrived to pick Maggie up, to say the change in

her shocked him was an understatement. He already thought she was perfect. He was definitely punching above his weight. She was intelligent, funny and a stunning natural beauty. She was everything he'd ever dreamed of. His jaw was on the floor.

It was a quiet drive, neither one of them saying much, each in a world of their own. Maggie was congratulating herself on a job well done. She felt every inch the sex object she thought he was looking for. She was disappointed that he was so shallow, after such an amazing first six months. But she'd show him what he'd be missing. She had every intention of dumping his shallow arse when they got home.

Mark was wondering what his parents would think of this alternative version of Maggie. He was taking her to meet them this weekend, so they could get to know each other. He thinks Maggie is the one, he's hoping to propose to her over dinner on Sunday night.

When they arrive at the farm, Maggie wonders what the hell is going on. It's hardly a romantic setting for their dirty weekend. An older couple comes to the door to greet them as they are getting out of the car.

'Mum, Dad, hi. This is Maggie' Mark hugs his parents, and his mum turns to smile at Maggie, giving her arm a squeeze as she takes her bag from her.

Maggie feels completely foolish, not to mention overdressed, as Mark's parents give her a guided tour around the pig farm!

DIRTY WEEKEND

Dean Wrigley

They had to wait for torrential rain. On their planet, life forms had evolved in an atmosphere heavily ladened with water vapour, which would condense onto their bodies, washing away the bodily waste products that seeped like pus from cysts, erupting from the surface of their leathery skin. Normally, it was neither painful nor considered ugly; it was simply the nature of their being. But certain things like alcohol and some foods could cause the process to be painful. But, whichever viscosity the fluid being excreted out was, it still stunk to high heaven.

The capsule caused an enormous crater as it landed with a thud into soggy ground. Inside the cabin, the crew was busily checking dials and measurements, attempting to determine when the window of opportunity would open and predict how long the adventurer had once outside.

If the water vaporisation level became too low, their skin cysts became hard and would keep the poisons they excreted, quickly building up to levels which usually resulted in instant death.

This had been the fate of many of the historic adventurers - whose portraits surrounded the middle of the craft - but the knowledge acquired during these failed attempts at first contact had allowed them to ascertain the limitations of their endeavour and the requirements for survival in the atmosphere of this strange, blue planet. Their world, called Stobotheria, is less than half the size of Earth but with a very deep ocean. By one of those strange cosmic quirks of fate, the distance of the planet from the star juxtaposed with the depth of the ocean and the force of the planet's gravity, ensured the planet tottered on the edge of an equilibrium where the evaporation rate of the ocean and the intensity of the rainfall allowed complicated life to evolve and flourish. Albeit vastly different to the life that had evolved on Earth.

A Stobotheria-wide lottery had been held for each mission, with the lucky winner offered the opportunity to go on a one-way trip to make first contact. Numerous attempts had already been made - every one of them a hero and every attempt ending in failure - but much had been learnt along the way.

Tazyjeb was the lucky winner for this epic, historic mission. It was fully expected that first contact would be accomplished on this voyage. Tazyjeb was the Stobotherian expected to achieve immortality.

Tazyjeb steadied themselves. They had looked over the dials and measurements for an hour after the capsule came to rest. They had made all the calculations and predictions. They were ready and had the Earth equivalent of 15 minutes before their cyst openings hardened too much and the poisons killed them.

First contact had to be made. Tazyjeb determined to be the first one to do it. A previous mission had determined there were stone structures, the sides of which were far too perpendicular and angled to have been produced by natural causes. It was surmised that these structures were made by an intelligent alien life form and, by finding one of these structures, first contact would be made.

The capsule had landed close to one of these structures and analysis of the air suggested alien life forms were within. Tazyjeb opened the door of the capsule and slipped outside. They took a deep breath of the air and was pleased that the oxygen level was similar to that of Stobotheria. Climbing out of the pit proved to be more difficult than expected. Tazyjeb could not get a firm grip with their feet in order to give them a good push up.

This was frustrating as time was slipping away. Eventually, with a mighty push, Tazyjeb reached the edge of the pit and used their hand to help in their ascent.

On reaching the top, Tazyjeb stood up and looked around. Unfortunately, an unexpected difference in the air's thickness and the viscosity of the raindrops caused their eyes to be unable to focus on anything and their vision was all a blur. Tazyjeb was determined, however, and carried on with their mission regardless of the effects. It was imperative; they had to make first contact.

Tazyjeb reached out and touched an upright, flat surface. This was definitely artificial! Following the flat surface by leaning against it, Tazyjeb could identify the direction of the mild smell and made slow progress towards it.

They could feel their skin cyst openings hardening and the poisons begin their work of intoxicating their body. 'Hold on for a few more steps,' thought Tazyjeb. Suddenly, Tazyjeb had a thought. One glimmer of hope. Perhaps the intelligent life forms they were close to contacting would have a cure for their predicament. Perhaps Tazyjeb would live!

With this hope, Tazyjeb forged onwards and came to an opening to a sheltered, artificial cave. Tazyjeb could hear voices inside, but inside was dry and far too dangerous for a Stobotherian. But in order to make first contact, Tazyjeb just had to go in. Death was certain. But immortality would last forever.

They entered the cave. Tazyjeb was in intense pain as their skin cysts quickly hardened and the poisons overpowered their body. But in the darkness, many pairs of eyes opened. Tazyjeb had done it. First contact between a Stobotherian and an Earthling had been achieved. A momentous occasion in the history of Stobotheria.

Far, far away, there were celebrations in the abodes of Stobotheria. There were Stobotheria-wide announcements. The name of Tazyjeb, the Great Adventurer, was written out in lights throughout every land. But Tazyjeb didn't see or hear any of it. They had fallen to the smelly, dirty ground, reaching out to the eyes coming towards them.

Tazyjeb's final struggled words were, 'I, Tazyjeb of Stobotheria, come in peace. Take me to your lea..' to which the reply was, 'oink, oink, oink' as the pigs ripped apart and feasted on Stobotherian flesh.

DIRTY WEEKEND

April Berry

Amanda and Peter had been looking forward to this weekend for a long time. Over the last 18 months, no one had been able to get away, but for them it had been April 13th 2019 since their last break. It wasn't for the want of trying, weekends booked and cancelled, disappointments, tears, frustration.

Before Covid, they had sometimes disagreed about when and where to go on weekends away, but this time they were both in harmony as to the destination. The hotel was booked and paid for. Plane tickets, passports, PCR tests booked and paid for, a small price to pay for the enjoyment that was coming their way.

Amanda and Peter were at the airport early, a novelty for them, ready and waiting for their flights to Paris, the most romantic city in the world- what a fantastic place for a weekend away.

Amanda had packed all the appropriate clothing, carefully planning every outfit for her and Peter, carefully chosen underwear, silky tops, tight fitting bottoms, all her favourite clothes.

Amanda's preference was for lots of light clothing. To her, there was nothing more satisfying than peeling off layer after layer of clothing, in anticipation of what was to come. Shaking herself out of her daydreaming suddenly as Peter was nudging her.

'Do you want a coffee and sandwich? It's still 2 hours to our flight and I'm starving' Considering her options, Amanda asked for a glass of wine. Staring at Amanda lovingly, Peter replied, 'are you sure? I don't want you to be asleep before teatime. We have looked forward to this for a long time.'

Amanda gave in. She knew Peter was so much more experienced than her at this.

As soon as they reached the hotel, Amanda and Peter were straight into the swing of things, meeting up with other likeminded friends they had a fantastic evening, but the anticipation of what was to come was mounting and Amanda was becoming more excited by the hour.

On the way back from the bar, Peter and Amanda were discussing the participants. This was the only thing that they perhaps disagreed on, both preferring different male and female participants.

They both had an animated sparkle in their eyes discussing their favourites, and it made this weekend even more special as it was the first time that the women had taken part and not been second class citizens and just been part of the audience. Previously, it was male only participation.

Peter was all for Anna and Walter, but Amanda's favourites were Lizzie and Dylan. However, after an animated discussion, they agreed to disagree.

Peter was up early on the Saturday morning, dressed and ready for action, he shook Amanda awake, desperate to be on their way to the action.

The day didn't disappoint. Amanda was highly satisfied with Lizzy's performance, whereas Peter was disappointed and Amanda couldn't resist teasing him all evening.

What did you really expect? She said on more than one occasion, as she showed Peter the pictures of Lizzie in the shower afterwards.

Sunday morning was a reversal of Saturday, with Amanda up and raring to go. Peter not so, as he expressed the fact that he hoped that today would bring more satisfaction for him than yesterday did. Amanda didn't care, she was still on a high from yesterday. They arrived at their destination. The venue wasn't open yet, so they hung around watching the action on the internet.

It was hard for them to work out who was who. Most people were covered in mud, slipping and sliding all over the place, different from yesterday, but even more exciting in what was to come.

Eventually, they were let into the venue and they didn't have long to wait for the action to come their way, but it wasn't who they thought it would be.

The noise around them rose to a crescendo as the cyclists entered the velodrome, caked from head to toe in mud. It was so hard to see who was who - the frantic sprint to the finish won by Sonny, neither Peter nor Amanda had predicted this, however they were still excited at being part of a piece of history. They had witnessed on this weekend the first ever edition of the Paris Roubaix cycle race for women and they were part of it.

The hell of the north - muddy, wet, caked dirt on every cyclist, crashes at every turn, the wettest Paris Roubaix in 19 years - possibly the dirtiest weekend of cycle racing that Peter and Amanda had ever seen.

SPARKLERS

Carolyn Ward-Daniels

They are strong, heavy words, but make no noise as they land on the page. Death. Blast. Landmine. Just thin ink on pristine paper. A letter that would deliver so much grief.

I crossed out the words 'I am sorry' I wasn't sorry at all. My pen poised as I dredged my mind of what to write to his family. Do I put 'It is with regret?' Well, it did damage a bloody good camera, but hey ho, well back to writing the death lines. I am tempted to write the whole gory scene, but writing isn't my job, like reporter Adam bloody Armitage. He would hide behind the armoured truck while I went into the battle zone to set up the camera. He would tell me which was his best side, wait until the light was flattering, tell me when to roll. 'Wait until I comb my hair before you film.' There he would pose dramatically, flinching at the cracks of live rounds in the distance, ending with his name, like it was all him. No mention of camera woman oh no, it was all him.

This day I had put my back up camera on the mudguard of the armoured truck before setting up my main camera on the tripod. I walked over to a low busted mud wall, posed and took a frame using my remote switch, then I stepped beyond the wall to see if it would make a better frame. That's when I saw it, just showing its killing edge through the dirt. The wind was blowing toward us carrying a whiff of Sulphur and I watched the crumbs of earth blow over the landmine. It was just two metres beyond the wall. I clicked the camera remote and went back. Armitage appeared,

'What's the light like?' He asked, not looking at me, 'are there any bullets flying?'

'Lights good, take a look at these positioning shots.'

He squinted at them and said, 'It looks better past the wall. If you see smoke behind me, try to get it in shot but mainly focus on me.'

'Shouldn't you have your helmet and flak jacket on?'

'It doesn't suit me, get me from the waist up and some background so people can tell I'm in a war zone, see the danger I put myself in to bring them the news.'

A soldier called over from the truck, 'We're moving out east in thirty minutes if you want to follow us to the big fireworks.'

Armitage wafted him away, saying, 'I'm fine sitting it out with the sparklers.'

'Well, be careful, this is unchecked territory, stick to the road we came in on.'

Armitage checked his face and hair in the wing mirror of the truck, then headed toward the battle buggered wall. He was only four metres away from me and I can remember feeling nervous. He turned and faced me, but shuffled backwards. I shouted, 'wait' he stopped, and I went to get my backup camera and I hurried the 50 metres to the truck. I grabbed the camera just as a deafening blast made me fall to the ground. The soldier ran from the truck, followed by two others. It was silent, almost slow motion. My camera and tripod were lying on the ground and I went to recover it. The three soldiers were standing by the broken wall shaking their heads at the bloody lump that was Armitage. One saw me and waved his arms for me to go. I could see what was left of Armitage and realised it could have been me. I also realised it needn't have happened. Then again, what was this war all about? Why am I here? All these miles from home, it's not my bloody war.

I had documented in pictures some horrific things. Bodies abandoned in bullet riddled rooms pretending to be home. Decaying humans lining the roads. I have become a different person. I am indifferent to death. We are not observing fireworks and sparklers; we are in the killing fields, the cities of death. You can smell it. Holding your nose and closing your eyes doesn't make it go away. It is around every corner here and I have gotten used to it. My veins are like earth wire zip wiring feelings straight out of me, bypassing brain and heart.

There are other reporters who will want to hire me and now I have built up this immunity of shock and horror I will carry on being invisible camera woman.

I am searching for despair, for that shot to capture desperate human life, to freeze-frame their hopelessness. A photograph to grab the attention of the faraway news bystander to try to fill their nostrils with the stench, their eyes with the carnage and their minds with a fog of fear. For them to be glad to be miles away from the killing fields farmed by soldiers.

I realise why I came here. It isn't for the pay cheque. I could earn more at home getting that shot of a tanked up celebrity stumbling out of a nightclub. It is weird what sells newspapers. I had come to show the plight of ordinary people, the ones without a voice who are being starved and slaughtered and think they are the forgotten ones. I am here to make sure they are not and in order to do that, I had to develop rhino skin.

Two years ago, on my first trip, I couldn't see for tears for a month and if I hadn't toughened up, I wouldn't be able to keep the hope alive for them.

SPARKLERS

April Berry

Ben's head jerked up, and his eyes darted all around the cellar. He was alert to every sound, his nerves jangling, sweat was pouring from him.

It did not really suit him, a life of crime, and Ben vowed that the last job was definitely that–the last. He had to hide the money somewhere until the proverbial dust died down, but his wife knew all his hiding places and having broken the promises he made to her to go straight, if she discovered the money, inevitably divorce would follow. Ben couldn't even justify to himself why he had agreed to the robbery, but it had given him the biggest payday of his life. Ben's eyes rested on the gigantic box nestled away on the shelf and immediately knew where he could hide the money. He had already rung in sick at work. In his present state, he really wasn't fit to do anything. Looking at his watch, he had over 8 hours to complete the task. Metaphorically patting himself on the back, he started to hide the money. All one hundred grand of his share from the heist.

Finally, just before 4pm, Ben had finished his task, and went upstairs, just in time to greet Gail, his wife, as she arrived home from work.

'Why are you home?' she asked, then looking at him said, 'never mind, you look dreadful.'

Across town, Mike was trawling the internet looking for a local firework display to take his girlfriend and her 2 small children to. He was looking forward to what was a bright future. Having had met Andrea about 6 months ago, Mike knew she was the one. He adored the kids and was thinking of asking her to marry him. Maybe if the bonfire and firework display were magical enough, he would do it there.

The doorbell rang. Mike jumped up to answer it, it was Gail, his sister. Following him into the living room, she saw the details of the local firework display glaring back at her.

'That's the reason I've come round,' she said. 'I'm thinking of having a firework party this year, a chance to get all the family together and a chance to get to know Andrea better. Ben is on a

late that day so I would need help though with setting it up.
'Mike hummed and awed, as he had plans of his own, but as
Andrea came out of the kitchen, overhearing the invite she said,

'Oh Gail, that will be lovely. I'm happy to help and I am sure
Mike will be too.'

'Brilliant,' said Gail, 'I've bought a large box of fireworks. The
only thing I've not bought are sparklers.'

'Not a problem, we can bring those and some bonfire toffee.
The kids will love it.' Mike was disappointed. It wasn't what he
had planned, but I suppose proposing will wait awhile. After all,
he thought, I'm here for the long haul. A few more weeks won't
make any difference. The morning of the 5th November was
bright, dry and sunny. Mike made his way over to his sisters to
help build the bonfire, glad to have some quality time with his
sister, a rarity these days, though Mike knew it was his own fault,
as he tried to avoid Ben, who he thought was a waste of space.
Bonfire built, Mike drove back home, waiting for Andrea to
arrive back from picking the children up from school. Just before
6pm, they set off to Gail's for the bonfire, which was already lit
when they arrived. Sending flames into the air, sparks from the
wood flying onto the lawn and giving off a wonderful heat to
combat what was a chilly evening.

Gail had wrapped potatoes in foil and was gently placing
them around the base of the fire. Mike could smell the aroma of
mushy peas laced with mint wafting from the kitchen. At the
bottom of the garden, Gail had cordoned off a section for
fireworks. Earlier, Mike and Gail had strategically placed the
fireworks, hopefully to give a magnificent display. They were
ready for Mike to light.

Mike's taper glowed bright red in the darkness, the light from
the bonfire giving him sufficient light to see the touch paper.
Firework after firework lit, made a weak puffing noise, sprayed
out a disappointing amount of glitter in the air and dying
pathetically. Gail was beside herself. Crying, she apologised
profusely to her brother and his girlfriend. She had so wanted
this to be a marvellous display. She had paid a fortune, and all
she had got were damp squibs. Mike consoled his sister, telling
her not to be upset. The sparklers, though, were a tremendous
hit with everybody.

Ben arrived home from his late shift, sauntering into the garden with a large box under his arm. He saw Mike throwing all the spent fireworks onto the bonfire. As the penny dropped what was happening, Ben, throwing the box of fireworks on the grass he'd bought to replace the box in the cellar, broke into a sprint that nearly ended with him joining the fireworks on the bonfire. Staring into the flames, he could just make out the silhouette of Turner's portrait burning brightly on the £20 notes he had spent hours hiding in those fireworks.

CHRISTMAS

Dean Wrigley

Last year I remember watching the lights on the silly plastic tree change colour from yellow to green to red to orange to blue to purple. It was something I'd done at this time of year for as long as I can remember.

Every few days, Uncle Dean would take Mummy Ellie out for an hour and return ladened with bags containing food. I would wait for him to deposit the bags in the kitchen and then flop to the floor, roll over, and allow him to tickle my tummy. It was our regular playtime. Mummy Ellie didn't enjoy playing with me.

Over winter, I noticed a change in Mummy Ellie. She lost a lot of weight and seemed to get weaker, and I annoyed her more often. I would bring her a mouse as a gift, but it just upset her even more. Uncle Dean would come round and either catch it or remove its corpse. No matter what I did, I couldn't please her. Uncle Dean would come round more often, bringing her little sweets that she always ate with a glass of water. It got to a point where he wouldn't even come in, he would just leave the bags outside the door and Mummy Ellie would pick them up when he had gone. I missed my tickles.

One day in early spring, Uncle Dean came around, put me in a carrier, and took me away. I thought I was being taken to the vets, but the journey only lasted a minute or so and I was carried into a room I didn't know. He let me out of the carrier and I crept out cautiously. Mummy Ellie was nowhere to be seen. I must have been cat-nabbed! I ran off and found somewhere to hide, to contemplate and take stock of the situation.

Eventually, I crept out and started exploring, looking for a way out. I found the cat flap, but it wouldn't open for me. I jumped on the window-sill. No escape there either. Nothing was familiar except my food bowls, food and biscuits. Did Mummy Ellie know I was here? Surely, she would look for me.

Uncle Dean was home every day. He hardly ever left my sight. He ignored my pleas to be allowed outside, and I had to do my toilet in the litter tray! Something I hadn't done for years!

Oh! the indignity of it!

One time I almost made an escape. It was nighttime. Uncle Dean was in bed, and I got a whiff of fresh air coming from the window in his room. I made a jump through the curtain and found the window open, but the gap wasn't wide enough for me to squeeze through. I had been thwarted in my escape attempt. But while I was at the window, I noticed there was something else in the air.

After a couple of weeks, he allowed me to wander into the garden. As I walked along, the air breezed into my face. I drew it in and I recognised a scent! It was the scent of home! Mummy Ellie was close by. I made a dash for it. Through the gap in the fence, over the road, and through the garden of the house opposite. And there I was in familiar territory! I knew exactly where I was, so I ran round to the door to tell Mummy Ellie I was home! She would be so pleased to see me again. Or so I hoped.

But when I got there, and she saw me, she got very upset. I heard her talking and a few minutes later, Uncle Dean turned up with the box and carried me away again. She was in on it! She didn't want me near her anymore. I was sad and resigned myself to my prison.

I was locked in the house again for a week or so, and then something strange happened. Uncle Dean let me go outside on my own. The cat flap started working for me and I could come and go as I pleased. One day, there was a knock at the front door. I heard a familiar voice and when I looked; I found Sister Jemma and Uncle Dean hugging, and I noticed a wetness in their eyes.

The familiar scent in the air seemed to fade day by day. One day, Uncle Dean brought in a cardboard box and put it in the living room. Gradually an aroma came from it that I recognised! It was the scent of home! Mummy Ellie was in that cardboard box! I scratched, and I scratched at it until Uncle Dean opened it and let me look inside. Mummy Ellie wasn't there. Uncle Dean closed the box and took it away.

One rainy summer day, Uncle Dean left the house dressed in black.

I have been here for many months now. The days are getting shorter and things aren't so bad anymore. Today, the cardboard box was fetched from a cupboard and something taken out of it. And now here I am, laying contentedly on the sofa, resting my head on Daddy Dean's leg, watching the lights on the silly plastic tree change colour from yellow to green to red to orange to blue to purple...

CHRISTMAS

April Berry

Clive stared longingly out of the window. Snow was falling heavily from the sky, swirling and dancing before it hit the ground. He stared at the garden, 'No playing out today then' he thought to himself.

He loved the taste of the flakes on his warm tongue, melting like a starburst, but his mum always scolded him when he came in from playing on the lane outside the house, covered in large white flakes, his coat soaking wet from running about, his legs sinking into the candy floss like drifts that gathered in the hedges in the lane outside his house.

He wasn't going to chance getting into trouble this year; he was a lot older and smarter than last year.

He continued to stare out of the window, watching people walking their dogs up the lane into the nature reserve, *his* nature reserve. He'd spent many a happy hour in the seasons of the last year. Spring was his favourite when all the wildlife woke up from their hibernation. He knew it was the time of year when all the babies were born, parents out of the nests foraging for food to sustain the life they had just brought into the world.

Clive was an inquisitive boy. His interest in nature, he thought, was commendable. Few boys his age had the knowledge he did about the wildlife. Clive especially loved the babies, his mum not so. This puzzled him, as he knew she loved animals.

The nature reserve was his playground. He was afraid of some of the dogs that arrived there, though. They always wanted to play with him, but he was wary of this. Some of them terrified him.

One of Clive's favourite hobbies was climbing trees. He knew the best ones to climb. Summer was the best season for this. The leaves provided him a hiding place, thick bushy canopy over the nature reserve, where he could observe the birds flying high above, tweeting and calling for a mate. Clive knew what this meant.

Clive knew that the snow heralded the arrival of Christmas.

There was always a tree in the house, brightly decorated with balls and lights. When he was younger, he adored the sparkling balls on the tree. He even tried to play football with them, his favourite sport, another time his mum scolded him.

Clive was lost in his memories. He didn't see his sister come up behind him and smack him on the head; he turned and whacked her back, just at the same time as his mum came into the room. 'Here we go' he thought, 'it's not enough I can't go out to play, my sister is now getting me into trouble!'

After Clive's mum has finished telling him off for bullying his sister, he turned back to the window. A slow smile spread across his face. The snow was stopping. Quite the chancer, Clive asked his mum if he could go out, never thinking for a moment she would relent, but she did. Clive could see her mouth moving, but he never heard a word she said. He was too excited to be going out into the garden, another of his favourite places.

'Stay in the garden,' his mum said, 'don't be going into the nature reserve. I don't want you coming back muddy and wet!'

Clive waited until his mum shut the door and he made a run for the nature reserve, 'She'll never catch me' he thought, 'she's old and can't run as fast as me.'

When Clive got into the reserve, he heard chirping. Some of the winter birds were hunting for food after the snowfall.

It looked beautiful in the reserve. The tree branches had all got ridges of snow on them that fell in a flurry to the floor whenever a bird landed on the branch. It intrigued Clive. He spotted the robin. This was his mum's favourite bird. She was always filling the bird feeder and watching those and the ones with blue feathers. He wasn't sure what they were called.

Suddenly Clive noticed a starling in the bushes. Just past the entry to the reserve, he stopped in his tracks. These were his favourite birds. Patiently, he watched the starling hop from the bush to the ground, which had been sheltered from the snowfall by the leaves. Clive didn't like the bush. Many a time, he'd been pricked and scratched as he was running through the reserve with his brother. The Starling used its beak to move the soil looking for worms; it had its back to Clive, so didn't notice he was watching.

All that was going through Clive's mind now was, 'All I need is a well-timed jump, just one extended claw and there is my Christmas Dinner!'

CHRISTMAS

Daizi Rae

Santa had the rosiest of rosy cheeks and a warm glow from the brandy. He was looking forward to a full tummy from the meat he was about to eat.

Donna and Blitzen sat on the side of the mountain, either side of Santa, watching the flames flickering from the open fire. Mouths watering, despite the guilt and the pain. Santa used a broken piece of the sleigh to rip off a slice of the cooked meat and offered it to Rudolph.

Donna looked at Blitzen in shock, outraged on her behalf, and turned to glare at Santa. 'Why does he get served first? I don't see why Blitzen shouldn't have all of that meat. It is her leg after all.'

Santa didn't even have the good grace to pretend surprise. He smirked at the two reindeer, reminding them that Rudolph was the only one of them that was still in one piece with no broken bones. 'I know who's naughty and who's nice,' he teased. Donna was so angry, she knew that if the crash hadn't broken her font legs, she would be up now and skewering his rosy faced fatness on her antlers.

Santa had them believe the sleigh crashed because of turbulence that made a present jump out of the sack blocking his vision. As if! More like the ever present aroma of brandy over the last few months.

In his stupidly jolly voice Santa slurred, 'Aren't the stars glorious this evening, ho ho ho! At least we're still alive.'

Donna glanced at Blitzen and they both shivered at the thought that Blitzen may not stay that way for long. They tried not to look at the pile of already stripped reindeer bones. They had died in the crash, and if the rest of them wanted to live... well, they had to keep their strength up.

'Mrs. Clause and the elves will look for us I'm sure.' Donna wasn't so sure. If she was Mrs. Clause, she'd have changed the locks and raised a glass to toast her freedom days ago. But she was too weak and cold to argue the point.

After the crash, they had survived for almost a week on

Christmas chocolate, mince pies, and candy canes. When they were all exhausted and help had not arrived, they'd made the awful decision to eat the flesh of the poor dead reindeer. Santa thought it rather delicious, if a little tough. Donna, Blitzen and Rudolph called it cannibalism.

Blitzen's leg was the last of the meat, so they all knew the end was coming, one way or another. Donna wouldn't put it past the jolly old lush to wake them in the morning to the news that Blitzen had died in the night, and it would be such a shame to let her death go to waste when her meat could save them a while longer to wait for rescue. 'The elves could find us and take us home any minute now, ho ho ho, isn't that right Rudolph.' Santa positively beamed, waving his fat arms at the nearest horizon. Donna was about to snort at him and his stupid exuberance when she spotted biscuits popping out of Santa's pocket as he waved his arms. It occurred to her that Santa really should have been much thinner by now, positively skin and bone. He's been holding out on them. The selfish old lush was still as fat as ever… Donna started dragging her antlers across the ground to sharpen them to a point. 'Hey Santa, come over here.'

AUTHORS CHOICE

Billy's Law - TJ Spencer

Denise Lewes sat straight, head held high. She didn't blink.

The Defence lawyer asked, 'Miss Lewes, on the day in question, what were you doing in Bradley, Lincolnshire?'

Denise speaks slowly, carefully, her speech not faltering. 'I went to Bradley intending to find Gavin Ragg.'

'And what was your plan when finding the deceased?'

'To teach him a lesson, that would change his mind about his actions.'

'What actions would those be?'

Denise took a deep breath and continued to explain.

'He brutally beat and killed a defenceless one-year-old dog, called Billy. Then he bragged about what he'd done online.'

'The law dealt with this incident, did it not?'

Denise spat back, 'The law gave Ragg a twelve week suspended sentence for killing that defenceless puppy!'

'Some would say it was just a dog.'

She furiously responded, 'Not just a dog, but a loving creature that had more entitlement to live than that thug!'

A rumble of anger came from Raggs family in the public gallery. Directed at Denise 'You're scum,' they roared.

Judge Sergent used his gavel to demand silence amid grumbles from the spectators and advised Denise, 'please continue Miss Lewes.'

Denise glared at the public gallery and yelled, 'You call me Scum!'

'Yes!' They yelled back in delight.

The judge's gavel went down once more as he demanded, 'Silence. I will remove anyone else that causes a disturbance from my courtroom. Please continue Miss Lewes, but please stick to the facts.'

Denise nodded 'Yes, your honor.' She paused and turned towards the defence lawyer as she spoke again, quietly at first.

'I wanted to give Gavin Ragg a taste of his own medicine.'

'Can you explain further?'

'I knew where Ragg lived. So I drove there and waited for

him. He appeared after a couple of hours, from the back door of his house, smoking a cigarette, not a care in the world.'

'Gavin Ragg?'

'Yes, he walked along the back path by his house, scot-free, not one day in prison for killing his girlfriend's poor, defenceless dog. I'd seen him on Facebook laughing at his actions, at the judge, the law, even laughing at his girlfriend for crying over the death of her puppy.'

'What did you do next, Miss Lewes?'

'I started my car and drove alongside him, opened my window to ask if he was Gavin Ragg. He turned and sneered yes at me. So what?'

'I asked him why he killed Billy, and he couldn't help but brag that he was being bad, barking, biting him. Said he tried to stop him, muzzling him with his hand. The puppy bit him, that's what he said. He made him angry, so he held Billy up by the scruff of his neck, then threw him on the floor. He wouldn't stay down, so he kicked him.'

'Liar.' Another shout went up from the public gallery.

The Judge brought down his gavel once more 'Silence. Remove that person from my court.'

Two burly security guards took the angry man by his shoulders, while he continued to rant. 'Bitch! Liar!'

'Take that man away. Anyone else want to disturb my court today? I will have you removed, too. Do you hear me.'

The public gallery glared back at the judge in sullen silence.

'Continue Miss Lewes.'

'Ragg kicked that poor dog to death. He bragged that he'd got away with it, even told me that Billy deserved to be dead. He told me to piss off and walked away from me.'

The defence lawyer led the conversation on, asking, 'Then what did you do, Miss Lewes?'

Denise spoke clearly, loud, somehow proud. 'I revved my engine, put it into gear, and drove toward him, straight at him.'

'So you were you angry at Mr. Ragg?'

'Angry! I felt sick at how little he cared about Billy, only saw him as a nuisance, a problem, a disposable object. Gavin Ragg killed that poor defenceless dog in cold blood.'

A gasp of shock was heard from the public gallery. The judge looked up, shaking his head as Denise Lewes heatedly continued.

'He knew what he was doing. He murdered Billy. So I drove my car at him. There was a wall stopping him from going anywhere. I remember him shouting and thumping the bonnet of my car hard enough to dent it. I drove at him again and again and again until he was still. All I could see was a body, the body of poor Billy. Dead!'

The defence lawyer asked with quiet disbelief, 'so you didn't see Ragg lying there?'

'I saw his body, but I also saw Billy's little body. A life for a life.'

Shouting went up from the public gallery, Denise Lewes ignored the shouting. She continued to speak. 'Gavin Ragg killed Billy. A living, defenceless animal that had as much right to life as he did. The law let him get away with murder. He would have killed again and again. So I took the law into my own hands. For Billy, I chose Billy's Law.'

'Billy's Law?'

'Yes, Billy's Law, for all animals, defenceless against cruel thugs like Gavin Ragg.'

'So, you took Gavin Raggs life in exchange for the life of Billy'

Denise looked both proud and defiant as she replied, 'Yes, I acted for Billy, in the name of Billy's Law.'

They sentenced Denise Lewes to twelve years in prison for manslaughter with diminished responsibility. Her supporters beat a path to the high courts, committing legal papers, addressing a new law to be built into justice.

Billy's Law.

AUTHORS CHOICE

Brave Bear - Jayne Love

I don't go out much, not just because of COVID-19, just because I don't go out much. I have a dog, though, named Bear, and he needs his walks.

I reach for his lead and harness. A few years back he would've been bouncing all over the place, excited to be going for a walk. He's nine now and way more chilled about it. So once his harness was on, I attach his lead and stuff my pockets with treats, not forgetting poo bags. It's the law nowadays, you know.

We ambled along the bank of the Beck that runs by our house, its noise so relaxing as it babbles its way along to who knows where. It was a dry day, not overly warm, at the beginning of spring. Bees are visiting the thistle flowers and buttercups. It's not long before the dreaded wasps are chasing me home!

As Bear and I enjoyed our walk, I spotted my seat. Well, it wasn't mine, I just called it that. It was a welcome rest for me, as walking was becoming a struggle for me these days. If it was a fine day, I would sit and have a cig and a rest before we ambled back home.

Today there was something on my seat. A Tesco bag for life, the hessian type. My first thought was 'lazy sods, there's a bin right there.' I picked it up to throw it in the bin, when I heard something inside it, like metal. My interest peaked. I looked inside. There was a purse, a mobile phone, keys, a packet of cigs, and what looked like an expensive lighter. The phone was on, but locked, so I opened the wallet. There was some money, a few credit cards and a driving license. The name on everything was Samantha Charles. The photo was of a woman in her early fifties I guessed, by the look of her. I did the math, and she was 53. Not a bad guess, I thought to myself. The address wasn't far away. I would call on my way home and hand it back. It slightly puzzled me about why she'd left it, but accidents happen.

I was sat having my customary cig, Bear sat staring at the thick, overgrown bushes behind me. Then he let out a long, low growl, his warning growl. I took hold of his collar as he stood, and his growls got longer and deeper. Something was bothering him, and he was letting whatever it was know he was not messing about. His hackles were up and I was getting spooked too. Bear wedged himself between me and the pathway in front of the bushes.

'If there is anyone in those bushes, I suggest you leave now before I let my dog off the lead.' I said, trying not to tremble as I spoke. There was a rustle of leaves, cracking of branches, and a figure ran out and scarpered down the ginnel. I couldn't see any features, but it was definitely a man.

This time fully spooked me, and I figured we'd been out of the safety of our house long enough. As I picked up the bag and stood up to go home, Bear pulled me as he ran into the bushes. I followed him as best I could; I didn't want to drop his lead in case there were more of them hiding in there. The next thing I knew, I was crashing to the ground, probably tripping over a twig. That made me swear. I looked up and Bear was sitting down, as if waiting for me. I turned round to see what I'd tripped on and saw a shoe. Then another shoe with feet in them, and legs. It was a woman!

Every inch of me said run, but that's totally not viable. I'm in my sixties, very overweight, running is not my forte. On touching her leg, it was warm; I checked she was breathing; it was low and shallow, but definitely there. There was blood on her sleeve, she was bleeding from her nose, her eye was swollen and closing up. She'd definitely been beaten, and badly. I cleared the leaves from around her face to help her breath better.

I needed to phone the police, but my phone was at home, and hers was locked. I had to leave her and go to the nearest house a couple of minutes away. I tied Bear to a branch and told him to 'guard and protect,' and left them both. The first house I came to didn't answer the door. At the second house, a woman answered. I quickly told her what I had found and asked her to call the police, which she did, and she also sent her husband back with me, just in case the man returned. I hadn't even thought of that happening.

When we got back, the woman, who I could now see was

Samantha, was groaning. I took her hand and told her, 'not long til help comes now,' as she squeezed my hand we heard the sirens getting closer. Bear had laid down beside us, watching the fella from the house. I wondered if he was the offender, but I was just being silly, wasn't I?

The ambulance took Samantha away to the hospital, and the police took my statement. They told me that this was the fourth attack in as many weeks, that Samantha was lucky that Bear and I had come along. The other victims had been raped, beaten and left for dead. The fact Bear and I had chosen this time and place for our walk was probably what stopped this being murder number four.

As I took my leave with Bear, I praised my brave boy and we wandered home via the chippy, where I rewarded him with his favourite chippy supper.

The Last Mascara - Carolyn Ward-Daniels

It was the needing to pee that woke Gloria and she reluctantly got out of bed. She felt relaxed though thinking, 'Ah Sunday, I can get back in bed and snooze until I'm ready.' Snuggled back in comfort and smiling into her soft pillow, the alarm screamed and she realised it was, in fact, bloody Monday. Her calm face now frowned, and she snatched the alarm to stop its horrible message and reset it for 5 more minutes. She checked in her mind that it really was Monday, and her beloved weekend was over. The alarm wailed again, and she was tempted to set another 5 minutes, but it just prolonged the agony.

She sat up and said, 'Shit!' three times and pushed herself into her routine, calling in to check on her hubby in the main bedroom. He was sound asleep. They didn't share a bed any longer as Jack tumbled and mumbled in arthritic pain most of the night and kept her awake. At the dressing table, she patted a little foundation on the signs of her liver spots and thread veins on her face. 'Just 3 months to go,' she spoke to the mirror, 'and retirement.' This cheered her up a little and she took up the hot curling tongs to scorch the goodness from her pretend blonde hair. Her mascara was about dry, so she would have to buy a new one. 'That will be my countdown,' she whispered. 'One last mascara will just do me until my last workday.'

They had been so frugal the past three years, especially since Jack retired. Their plans of having special holidays were getting closer, and they saved every penny. They wore clothes until worn out. They bought food and necessities when on offer. Whilst putting a wave into her hair, she thought, 'When I retire, I won't pay to have blonde highlights. I will go naturally grey like Jack.' Gloria heard him groan in pain as he creaked his way to the bathroom. He opened her door to say 'Good morning,' and a whiff of Deep Heat entered too.

'Bad night, love?'

Jack nodded. 'Are you taking the car today?'

'Yes, love, I need to call at Tesco for a mascara after work and I tell you, this will be my last one. It should take me to July and then I don't care.'

He smiled through his pain and hobbled downstairs. He got the toaster out, as he hadn't taken to the cheap unbranded cereal Gloria had bought. All this frugality was making life miserable. Still, it wouldn't be long now before they could let loose and get away. He thought about the boating holiday they dreamed of and was doubtful about being able to get on and off a boat with his unreliable knees. Sightseeing anywhere would literally be a stumbling block.

Gloria filled her cereal bowl and pulled an uncertain face. It wouldn't have improved since yesterday. Jack saw her hesitate and said, 'I wouldn't get that again, love it doesn't taste wonderful.'

'True, well, soon we shall go out to brunch a couple of times a week and at least once a month we shall go out for dinner.' She noticed the cuff of her blouse fraying and pulled her cardigan sleeve down.

Jack buttered his toast and, glancing at her, said, 'You always look smart when you go to work. I might miss that if I'm honest.'

'I won't become a bag lady, but I'm telling you I am buying my last mascara. Nearly six years ago, I should have retired. I could have cried when I got that letter telling me I had to work until I was 66.'

'I know, love,' he said, patting her hand. She looked at his kind face, but she could always tell when he was in pain. It showed in his eyes. 'Still,' she comforted, 'at least we will have 6 years of extra savings. The first holiday could be on the Norfolk Broads. Hire one of those posh cruisers you liked in the brochure.'

Jack smiled weakly at her enthusiasm, but didn't know if he could cope with their dream holiday. They kissed each other goodbye and Gloria left after striking yesterday from the calendar.

The office was manic. Gloria was so busy and whilst she could have done with another day in the week to combat the workload, she couldn't wait to count it away. She never left work on time, and the stress always travelled home with her.

Even as she paid at the till, her breathing was still rapid and by the time she got back to the car, she felt like she was trembling all through her body. It was a white knuckled drive home; she didn't like this feeling at all. Jack heard the familiar sound of the car pulling into the drive and went to put the kettle on. He then heard the car horn. He rushed outside to find Gloria slumped at the wheel.

One week later, Jack shuffled into the undertakers with the new mascara he had found in Gloria's handbag. With a tremble to his voice, he said, 'Would you be so kind as to have someone put this mascara on my wife's lashes? She never went out without it.'

Topless Tease - Dean Wrigley

Mrs. Goldsmith looked at the consequences of easing her frustrations and felt no regrets. Her spleen well and truly vented. She turned and walked back into her home.

A few moments later, Michael's car entered their new road, drew up to their new house, and turned into their new driveway.

He got out of his car and went into his new home. His new wife, Ginny, was in their new kitchen. The kettle had just boiled, and she was about to pour the water into the mugs.

She spoke to her husband, 'Look what just arrived from Amazon. I've been upstairs hoping the delivery man would arrive before you got home and he brought us this just ten minutes ago! Do you like it?' she pointed at their new kettle. She looked at Michael and saw his hands were empty. 'Did you remember to pick up some milk from the shop?' she asked him.

'Oh, no! It completely slipped my mind. I'll nip out and get some now before I get settled,' said Michael.

'Ok, hun, kiss first,' she said, 'I'll leave the mugs for you to finish when you get back.'

Michael kissed her and then went out to his car again. He backed it out of the driveway and was just about to set off when something caught his eye. There appeared to be a huge, messy mark on the wall. He carried on to the shop, bought some milk, and returned home. He slowed down as he was about to turn into his driveway and looked at the house wall again. There was definitely the mark of a freshly splattered egg on the wall.

Someone had thrown an egg at their house today. Recently, in fact, because it was still dripping. Puzzled, he went into the house and completed making their mugs of tea, stirring slowly while pondering about what had happened. It was a mystery.

An hour earlier, things were getting heated in the Goldsmith's house. The new people across the road had finally got to Mrs. Goldsmith's goat. Actually, the new man was fine. He had introduced himself to Mr. & Mrs. Goldsmith within the first few days of them moving in and seemed a decent chap. No, it was the wife who had ignited Mrs. Goldsmith's fire. She had been watching afternoon television with her little grandson Charlie, playing quietly near the window. Now and then he would giggle. She loved the sound of her grandchild's laughter. Suddenly, Charlie said, 'Nanny, that lady in the window is funny. She doesn't have any clothes on.'

'Um, what lady?' she questioned, and went over to where Charlie was sitting. When she looked across the road towards the house opposite, she saw the back of their new neighbour's head disappear into the shade of an upstairs room. A few moments later, the woman appeared at the window again, and Mrs. Goldsmith couldn't believe her eyes.

Their new neighbour was practically hanging out of the window, looking down the road whilst completely topless. Mrs. Goldsmith was lost for words. 'Come away from the window, Charlie, and play in your room. Now, please,' she said sternly.

Her grandson started to blub as he moved away. 'Go on, do as I say. Into your room now, please.' Mrs. Goldsmith sat at the table and watched her new neighbour's house. At the sound of every motor engine, this woman would appear at the window, brazenly flashing her tits for all and sundry to see. It was outrageous behaviour in such a respectable area.

You wait until Mr. Goldsmith hears about this. There'll be words to the Parish Council, no doubt. The neighbour appeared time and time again with absolutely no shame. Finally, Mrs. Goldsmith flipped. She had had enough. She stomped through the rooms in her house, wondering how she could show her displeasure. Eventually, a course of action was decided upon. First she checked in Charlie's room to see he was playing quietly with his Lego. Then she went to the kitchen, grabbed an egg, stormed out of her front door and crossed the road before hurling the egg with all her might towards the neighbour's window. She wasn't a great shot, and the egg splattered into a million pieces on the wall beneath.

Michael completed making the teas and carried Ginny's upstairs to their computer room. When he got there, he found his wife sat at the computer completely topless, as usual.

'I've spent the entire afternoon refining my CV and filling out thousands of job applications online,' she said as she took the mug from her husband's hand.

'I'm very proud of you,' he said honestly, and kissed her forehead. 'Did you know there are the remains of an egg splattered on the wall?' he asked.

'Our wall?' she inquired.

'Yes, on our wall, out here, below this window,' he said.

'When did that happen?' she asked as she rose from the computer and looked out the window again.

Michael watched her and smiled as the mist cleared.

Loving a Stranger - Jayne Love

As Ali glanced over the breakfast table, she looked at her partner of twenty-two years and smiled. She thought back to when they first met.

Ali wasn't a party girl, but her friends dragged her along to an online meet up in the Gay Village in Manchester. Ali was on the shy side, not confident around people she didn't know, so this was a big thing for her. She tried not to get noticed. She was on the chubby side with glasses and not, in her opinion, a pretty girl.

As she glanced around the room in the last pub of the evening, one girl stood out from the crowd. And wouldn't you know it, she made her way over to Ali's group of friends.

'Hi, I'm Reni,' she said to Ali's group of friends. They all introduce themselves in turn. When it came to Alis' turn, she dropped her head.

Looking at the floor as she shyly whispered, 'I'm Ali.'

Reni joined the group for what was left of the evening, and they all had a fun time. As they were all getting ready to leave, Reni asked Ali for her number. Surprised but flattered, Ali put her number in Reni's mobile and gave it back to her. Reni rang it. 'Just checking,' she said, 'and you've got mine now. I'll call you sometime. We can make a date if u want.' Ali smiled.

In the taxi home, Ali smiled to herself, thinking, she won't phone, she was just being nice. Then her phone rang; It was an unsaved number. Normally she didn't answer those calls, but some instinct told her to, so she did.

'Hi its Reni, can u come back to the pub? You've left your coat behind.'

Ali asked the taxi driver to go back and when she got there, Reni sent the driver on his way.

That was their first meeting and to be honest, there didn't seem to be anytime at all in between then and them becoming a serious item. They moved in together three months after meeting and everything was good.

Ali smiled, thinking of their first kiss. Reni had slid her arm around Ali's waist, putting her hand in the small of her back, and pulling her in close. Ali had let out a small gasp. That kiss was the beginning of a beautiful, mutually passionate, caring life together.

Reni was a photographer and travelled a lot. Ali was a retail manager in a supermarket and worked too much. But they found the right balance, so they got quality time together. Twenty-two years later and they had never spent a night apart.

Ali buttered a slice of toast and put it on Reni's plate. 'Marmalade, Honey or Golden Syrup?' she asked.

Reni looked at her and said, 'Beanz means Heinz.'

Ali smiled and went to the cupboard. She heated a can of beans and put them on the now cold toast, and passed the plate to Reni, who chuckled, 'They make me fart.' Ali laughed, and then the reality hit her and she had to fight to keep the tears at bay.

Two years ago, their life together changed forever. Reni had been diagnosed with Alzheimer's. It was a shock, but the changes were small and manageable in the beginning. She had got progressively worse over the last six months though. It was so hard for them both. Reni was only sixty-six.

Two years on and the moments Reni was actually herself were fewer and fewer. Ali wasn't ready to lose the love of her life. She wasn't ready to be alone, or for the emptiness of life without Reni.

She didn't care that she had to sell their house to pay for the care home, because it wouldn't really be home without Reni, anyway. Reni, being safe and cared for by professionals, that mattered.

'They're coming from the care home today, Reni. They'll be here any time now.' Ali said, trying to check her emotions.

The doorbell rang.

Ali walked slowly to the door. She ran her hand across the back of Reni's shoulders as she passed her.

Reni spoke quietly and clearly, 'I've always loved you Ali, I never want to forget that.'

The tears fell from Alis' eyes and the doorbell rang again.

AUTHORS CHOICE

Still Life - Carolyn Ward-Daniels

I cannot sign a painting when I think it's finished. I have to ignore it for a while and then I can view it with fresh eyes. If I then believe it is finished, I will put my name to it. My last painting is ready for that consideration, as Martin forbade me to paint for two weeks. Not being allowed to paint unsettles my mind and makes me angry, which I have to keep wrapped up inside. He said I had lots of chores to do. It has been a twenty-year chore being married to him. So back to my viewing. Now he's out of the way.

I checked my picture against the photograph I had painted it from. I prefer to paint plein-air but to capture the beauty of a moment in the formation of a wave can only be done with a camera, indeed several attempts to get the right frame. The perfect light, the crescent, a statue before the tumble. When you've captured that, you can attempt to paint it.

The challenge of choosing solid colour, mixing them and landing them on a naked canvas and replicating that image is a rewarding feeling. It stills my bad thoughts; the concentration absorbs my anger. It is difficult to paint something that moves and constantly changes form like sauntering clouds. The other gripe about painting plein-air is that it takes time travelling, setting up an easel, fighting a breeze or rain and then getting into trouble with Martin because the hoovering didn't get done and his shirts weren't ironed. He thought he could prevent me from painting by giving me housekeeping money in tiny amounts so I can't buy art materials. It makes it difficult with a man who demands steak three times a week. But I am thrifty, I can save and I go without luxuries myself, I go without steak for one.

So the beach painting I am happy with. The curling wave nearly transparent. The flicks of spray give it movement and the froth on the hem of the retreating waves look like you could paddle in them. I have made the pebbles shine like jewels; the colours are perfect. I can sign and date this now. Martin won't see it and nag me for painting instead of mowing the lawn and cleaning his golfing shoes.

I can now start my new painting. I like still life; it doesn't move about. I adore the smell of oil paint and linseed oil, but I need to work in acrylics today as they dry quickly. I put a glob of cadmium red and a tiny pimple of black on my palette to begin with. I must get the correct depth of colour of that pool before it dries, but there is a fair amount of it to stay liquid. Maybe I'll just dip my brush in it and put a true colour sample on the scrap paper to check the red against. I don't want to disturb the pool on the floor. It has such a wonderful depth and sheen to it. I'll take it from the back of his head. Oops just trod on your finger, Martin, but you won't feel it, and it was the last time you'll wag it at me.

Who's Lucy - Dean Wrigley

Ginny had overheard Michael talking to himself in the bathroom. It had played on her mind all night and there was no other option; she just had to ask him, 'Who's Lucy?'

Michael looked at Ginny, his face turning ghostly white. Ashen. 'Sit down. I'll tell you,' he said.

They sat at the dining table. Ginny, suddenly feeling vulnerable, searched for answers in her husband's eyes.

Michael began. 'You know I lost my virginity at 15?'

She nodded. 'Well, it was with my girlfriend at school.'

'Lucy?' asked Ginny.

'No. With Faye,' said Michael. 'Me and Faye were in the same class. We had just started as an item. We thought we were in love. Thought we were grown-up. Thought we knew what we were doing... Nine months later Lucy arrived.'

Ginny took a sharp intake of breath. 'A daughter!' she exclaimed. 'You've never said. And Chrissy never told me she has a sister. So Lucy would be, what, in her late thirties by now? Where is she?'

Michael looked down. 'Chrissy never met her,' said Michael.

'Chrissy never met her? How come?'

'Well, maybe they met once or twice, but she was far too young to remember. She would have been only three.'

Michael's voice was steady and true, but when their eyes met again, Ginny saw tears glistening.

She took his hands. 'Oh sweetheart, what's wrong? I'm surprised you've kept it from me. But I forgive you. Why the tears? Where is Lucy now? Do you know?'

Michael nodded and sighed. Breathing deeply, he closed his eyes and continued. 'When Faye's parents found out she was pregnant, they moved away. They moved miles away and wouldn't let Faye and me have any contact. But my parents were pleased they had gone. It gave them a chance to convince me it was for the best. They didn't want my future to be hindered by a baby. I went with it. I was a silly, selfish teenager and I didn't want to be a dad at 15.'

'Oh, Michael,' said Ginny sternly. 'That's not like you at all.'

'I know, but I was different back then. I didn't even know that Lucy had been born until years later when I received a letter from Faye asking for money.'

'I supported her until she was 16, left school and started working. When she was 17, she passed her driving test, and I bought her a second-hand car. She came to see me in it.'

'Wow! And you'd never met her before?'

'No. Sally didn't mind. She encouraged it. Wanted us to welcome her into our home. Chrissy was just a toddler. It was nice. Lucy bought her a little teddy.'

'We met up with her once again. She was with her boyfriend. What's his name? Oh, it'll come to me. But that was the last time we met. Clark. His name was Clark. Strange choice for a forename.'

'Well, Superman's name is Clark! What happened to Lucy? How come you didn't see her again? Did Faye make a fuss? Or Faye's parents?'

Michael shook his head, 'No, nothing like that... I wish it were.' He took another deep breath.

'Lucy really suffered with her periods. For a couple of days every month, she turned into a monster, according to Clark. He usually steered well clear of her when she was in one of her moods.

On this winter's night she was supposed to stay at his place, but the red mist appeared, alcohol fueled. They had a blazing row, and she got in her car and drove off in a snow blizzard.'

'Oh my God! Drunk? In a blizzard?'

'Yeah. Clark said he tried to stop her, but she wouldn't listen. He even called the police but couldn't tell them the registration number. I don't blame him. Why would he need to remember that? She overtook a car that was going too slow for her. Lost control of her car and drove it into a tree. She died instantly.'

'Oh my God!'

'Clark rang to tell me what had happened. It was so cruel. She was only 19.'

'Did you hear from Faye?'

'Not straight away. I went to the funeral. Only me - Sally didn't come. Faye just thanked me for going. And I've not heard from her since. Not that I want to.'

'Wow! I need a cup of tea. So Lucy would have been 38 by now. When was her birthday?'

'Yesterday,' said Michael.

MEET THE AUTHORS

Carolyn Ward-Daniels: Carolyn was born on the Derbyshire, Nottinghamshire border and has lived in both counties in equal measure. She completed four full-time years at college to leave with a degree in industrial art and design specialising in interiors. Her working life has been in this design field and any spare time after sleeping is spent writing and painting. Her first novel 'August' has full 5 star reviews and her second novel 'Flint' hit the top ten books on Amazon. She has started to write the sequel to 'Flint'. Her weakness is cake, vodka, books and guitars in that order.

Dean Wrigley: An ageing lyricist and cat lover finally rediscovering his love of the written word.

Jayne Love: Jayne was born in Harrogate, and bought up in Studley. She now lives in Manchester but remains always proud of her Yorkshire roots and accent - even if that accent is now peppered with Mancunian colloquialisms. Jayne lives with four cats, all of whom she loves to bits.
Jaynes Rottie, Rufus sadly passed away as we went into publication. RIP Rufus - Forever in our hearts.

Gerry O'Keeffe: Writer, podcaster and all round Sci-Fi and Crime Fiction geek. Gerry also writes under the pen name Benny O'Caffery.

TJ Spencer: Trace (TJ) Spencer, creative diva with nibs of steel. Once upon a time, a girl was given a piece of paper and a pen, and asked to write a story. That's where her creative, imaginative adventures began.

Elaine Morris: Elaine is a Yorkshire lass, born and raised in Bradford, gradually moving in a southerly direction via Sheffield and Derbyshire until settling in Nottinghamshire 30 years ago. She had a satisfying career nursing in the NHS, before moving into IT and then retiring in 2013. Since then she has had a new career in volunteering, locally and internationally, in large multi sports events. When not on the move, she can be found knitting and watching TV. Like many people, she felt she had a story within her. While writing for Bare Books, she came to realise she didn't enjoy the process of writing and would rather be knitting!

April Berry: April is a Yorkshire lass who moved south 25 years ago and has stayed put. She is mum to 2 fur babies, and can often be found cycling round Nottinghamshire in her spare time or listening to Motown or Soul music, sometime both at the same time. An avid reader since she could hold a book, Enid Blyton in childhood, moving on to the Constable books, John Grisham, James Patterson and Lee Child amongst her favourite authors. The day jobs have concentrated around food with a side way shift to employment issues latterly. April never considered writing until just recently, cajoled and chivvied into it by her co-presenter on Bare Books podcast, where, along with Daizi, she can be found reviewing all that is good from Independent authors.

Daizi Rae: I was born and raised in Nottingham. Well, apart from the time I ran away to the seaside, changed my name and got a tattoo. Every girl needs at least one adventure! I always claimed to have been raised by Enid Blyton and her Famous Five, Secret Seven, and Mallory Towers. Moving on to binge on the likes of Stephen King, Clive Barker and Dean Koontz as an adult. You can find me on the Bare Books Podcast which highlights and amplifies independent authors, along with a wonderful dose of story telling.

BONUS: AND IN MY DREAM

Dean Wrigley

The little abandoned cat had chosen me for his human, and I welcomed him into my home. I would lay on the carpet and he would rub his head against my hand and my fingers would scratch his body through his fur. We were best buddies.

It has been many years since Blazy crossed the Rainbow Bridge and while my waking memories of him remain strong and I often smile when he comes to mind, that physical presence is no longer there.

But recently I had a dream.

And in my dream I was lying on the carpet looking across the room at Blazy curled up sleeping.

And in my dream I saw him open his eyes, and he saw me lying there on the floor.

And in my dream I watched him rise from his slumber; stretch his legs and start walking towards me.

And in my dream I reached out my hand, closed my eyes and I waited...

And in my dream, or was it in reality, my heart was filled with euphoria as his body rubbed against my hand and my fingers felt through his fur once more.

And not just as if it were in a dream, but for real. For real!

In my dream, my mind had expected a feeling and had dragged it up from the depths of my memory and awarded me something that touched my soul. Not just the imagined feeling, but the real feeling. Something it could not have possibly given me during my waking hours.

Printed in Great Britain
by Amazon

34270020R10111